TWO-GUN DEVIL

TWO-GUN DEVIL

Jackson Cole

Chivers Press • G.K. Hall & Co.
Bath, England • Thorndike, Maine USA

This Large Print edition is published by Chivers Press, England, and by G.K. Hall & Co., USA.

Published in 2000 in the U.K. by arrangement with Golden West Literary Agency.

Published in 2000 in the U.S. by arrangement with Golden West Literary Agency.

U.K. Hardcover ISBN 0-7540-4015-1 (Chivers Large Print)
U.S. Softcover ISBN 0-7838-8847-3 (Nightingale Series Edition)

The text of this Large Print edition is unabridged.
Other aspects of the book may vary from the original edition.

Set in 16 pt. New Times Roman.

Printed in Great Britain on acid-free paper.

British Library Cataloguing in Publication Data available

Library of Congress Cataloging-in-Publication Data

Cole, Jackson.
      Two-gun devil / Jackson Cole.
         p.   cm.
      ISBN 0-7838-8847-3 (lg. print : sc : alk. paper)
      1. Hatfield, Jim (Fictitious character)—Fiction.
      2. Frontier and pioneer life—Texas—Fiction.
      3. Texas Rangers—Fiction.   4. Large type books.   I. Title.
PS3505.O2685 T96   2000
813'.54—dc21   99–054773

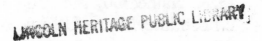

CHAPTER ONE

From Alto on the west to Marton, the railroad town north of Escondida Valley, runs a trail that winds and slithers around the mountainside like a tortured snake. To the north are overhanging cliffs. To the south is a sheer drop of hundreds of feet to where a rock-studded stream foams in the depths of the gorge below. The trail is narrow, with barely room for two vehicles to pass, and the turns are sharp, the lip of the canyon wall broken and crumbling.

About two miles east of Alto, where the hills begin, another trail joins the Marton Trail, a trail that runs from El Paso on the Mexican Border.

Riding east by north on the El Paso Trail, Jim Hatfield pulled his great golden horse to a halt at the forks, hooked one leg over the saddle horn and rolled a cigarette with the slim fingers of his left hand. For some minutes he smoked thoughtfully and surveyed the forbidding terrain ahead. He pushed back his wide 'J.B.' and rumpled his thick black hair. His rather wide mouth quirked at the corners as he spoke to his horse.

'A rather fitting gateway to the section we're heading for, Goldy,' he remarked. 'One little slip on that snake track ahead and you'd starve to death before you hit bottom. Well, guess we'll have to chance it. About twenty miles to go yet before we can put on the nosebag. Not even a scrap of chuck hereabouts for an old grass burner like you. Nothing but rock, and that's sort of hard to chew. So let's get going.'

He settled himself in the saddle once more and hooked his double cartridge belts a little higher around his lean waist. Broad shoulders swaying, he rode easily along the Marton Trail.

Soon the long slope to the south gave way to a perpendicular rock wall against which the stream, far below, foamed and thundered. Hatfield, riding the outside of the trail, glanced into the awful depths beneath his elbow and moved Goldy a little farther in. The broken lip of the cliff was not good riding surface.

Hatfield rode slowly. It had been a hard pull from the desert to the southwest and Goldy was entitled to take it easy for a spell.

For a couple of miles the trail was almost level, then it developed a downward trend that increased in steepness as they bore farther and farther into the hills. They topped a rise and a long, fairly straight stretch came into view. About a mile distant, where the crowding north cliff bulged outward sharply, the trail seemed to leap off into space. Hatfield knew the bulge must mark the site of a hairpin turn.

A few minutes later, Hatfield lifted his head and turned in the saddle. From behind

2

sounded a rumble of wheels. Another instant and the long, lean heads of two big and powerful mules bulged into view over the crest of the rise. Behind the mules rose a buckboard, careening and rocking. The team and the vehicle came charging down the slope at a dead run.

'For the love of Pete!' Hatfield exclaimed, crowding Goldy close to the outer lip of the trail, 'Is that jigger plumb loco?'

On came the buckboard, reeling and bouncing, sparks streaming from its grinding tires. On the seat was a single occupant.

The racing vehicle roared past and Hatfield exclaimed again. The occupant of the seat was a slender, white-faced girl. Hatfield saw that the end of a broken rein, whipping wildly about, was lashing the frenzied off-mule at every leap.

Hatfield's voice rang out, 'Tail, Goldy, trail! We've got to catch that thing before it makes the turn. They'll never take it. The whole shebang will go into the canyon. Trail!'

Instantly the great golden horse shot forward, irons drumming the ground, his glorious black mane tossing in the wind. He slugged his head above the bit and literally flashed down the long slant of the trail.

As he estimated the distance toward the turn, Hatfield's mind worked at lightning speed. He had to either halt the runaway before it reached the turn or somehow get it

3

around the sharp curve. How in blazes to do it! Goldy's great weight and strength could force the flying mules in toward the cliff, but that was the very thing that wouldn't do. The mules, though mad with fright, would continue to hug the cliff, and they would possibly make it around the bend. Horses would very likely fall, but not the sure-footed mules. But when they went around, the buckboard would swerve outward, and as the mules took the turn, it would be shot from the trail like a stone from a catapult. The mules must be forced to the outer lip, but how could it be done. There was no room for Goldy to pass the buckboard on the inside, and were he on the outside of the team, it would be impossible to drag the mules close enough to the outer edge to save the vehicle and its occupant. There was only one thing to do, and Hatfield knew he would be taking a frightful gamble with death. But there was no time to lose; the bulge was racing toward them like a living thing.

Behind the panic-stricken mules, the buckboard was fairly flying, but steadily the great sorrel closed the distance. His straining nose came level with the rear wheels then drew up to the seat. For an instant Hatfield contemplated snatching the girl from the vehicle, but the risk was too great. Should the sudden shifting of his weight throw the sorrel off balance they would be almost sure to go over the lip. He shot a glance at the bend; it was flowing toward them at a frightening rate.

'Hang on!' he shouted to the girl as Goldy forged farther ahead. Now he was breasting the haunches of the run-aways. Another instant and he was almost to the off-mule's shoulders. Hatfield rose in his stirrups, measured the distance with his eye and leaped in a headlong dive. He heard the girl scream her terror, then with a shock that almost drove the breath from his body, he landed draped across the mule's withers.

Under the impact of his weight, the animal all but lost its footing. By a miracle of agility it recovered and with a maddened squeal dashed on, Hatfield swaying and slipping, his fingers groping for the bit ring and the cheek-piece. He got a finger into the ring, with his other hand he gripped the stout leather strap that was the cheek-piece. Now everything depended on the strap being able to withstand the strain. If it broke, he'd be at the bottom of the canyon in a matter of seconds. Tightening his grip and thrusting his finger farther into the ring, he hurled his body sideways, letting all his weight come upon ring and strap, jerking the mule's head down and around.

Again the animal nearly fell, but again it recovered. Hatfield, dangling, his feet striking the surface of the trail one instant, flinging upward the next, kept swaying his body outward. And as he did so, the mule was forced to veer away from the cliff, dragging its team-mate with it.

Nearer and nearer the ragged lip swerved the flying hoofs. Hatfield felt himself swing dizzily in empty space. Beneath him, a thousand feet and more, was the white water thundering over black rocks, a vision of terror. Then he was over the surface of the trail again, and directly ahead was the hairpin turn!

He heard the clang and scrape of the mule's slipping irons, the clashing and grinding of the buckboard against the cliff as it swung inward. Then as the mules took the bend, it careered outward. Out and out, nearer and nearer the broken, crumbling lip. Let one wheel go over the edge and ruin was certain. The tires screeched their protest. The mules floundered, recovered, floundered again, and recovered yet again. Their lean heads craned inward away from the horrible depths, their scrambling hoofs sent fragments of rock hurtling downward. The inner side of the buckboard rose high in the air, until Hatfield was sure it would capsize. Then with a crash and a thud it righted, and went rolling down the straight trail beyond the bend, crowding against the haunches of the sobbing mules, whose gait quickly slacked to a shamble. Hatfield, his feet now on solid ground ran lightly beside them till he forced them to a halt. He was bruised and battered, his hands were bleeding and his breath came in great

6

gasps. Still gripping the cheek-piece, he stepped back and stared at the girl on the buckboard seat.

She was small and slender, her big blue eyes still clouded with fright, her short curly brown hair wildly wind-tossed. Some color was coming back into her pale cheeks and her sweetly curved lips were resuming their normal vividness.

'Usually come down the hill that way?' Hatfield panted. 'Exhilarating, but I don't recommend it.'

'It would have been more than exhilarating had it not been for you,' she replied with a shudder, her voice trembling slightly. 'I was going to jump before we reached the bend, but the chances are I'd have gone over the cliff or broken my neck.

'There are no words to thank you for what you did, so I'm not going to even try,' she added. 'You risked your life to save mine—I still can't understand why you weren't killed. It was the most daring thing I ever saw or heard tell of.'

'Oh, there wasn't anything much to it,' Hatfield said lightly. I just had to hang on till the mule couldn't take it any longer. Now I'll see if I can get this broken rein patched up.'

He soothed the trembling mules for a moment with voice and hand and turned his attention to the rein.

'Reckon it will hold now till we get to town,'

7

he said a little later. 'I suppose you're headed for Marton?'

'That's right,' she answered. 'My father will meet me there. He owns a farm in the valley south of Marton. I'm Verna Hardin.'

Hatfield's eyes narrowed slightly as she pronounced the name and he abruptly recalled the parting words of Captain Bill McDowell when he dispatched his Lieutenant and aceman to Escondida Valley.

'So far as I've been able to ascertain, the hombre chiefly responsible for the hell raising over there, who runs the section politically and otherwise and the man who will very likely give you the most trouble, is an old shorthorn by the name of John Hardin.'

However, Hatfield merely acknowledged the introduction and supplied his own name. He whistled to Goldy, who had halted behind the buckboard and was regarding the whole affair with a slightly bored air. The sorrel trotted forward and paused alongside him.

'Reckon we might as well be ambling,' Hatfield suggested. 'I'll ride along with you. You're not afraid to handle the team now?'

'No,' Verna Hardin replied firmly. 'If I didn't drive now, the chances are I never would again, after the scare I got. The rein broke just the other side of the rise. I've a notion when the loose end whipped around it struck the mule on the nose or in the eye. He immediately proceeded to run away and the

8

other got frightened and ran with him. There was nothing I could do.'

'Lucky you kept your head and didn't try tugging on the other rein,' Hatfield remarked approvingly. 'If you had, there would have been a good chance of veering the whole shebang over the cliff. Feel all right now?'

'I realized I mustn't do that,' she agreed. 'Yes, I'm all right, but I'll be very glad to have you ride with me. I want you to meet my father; he'll have plenty to say to you.'

At a good pace they proceeded down the trail, the girl handling the now thoroughly subdued team with a deftness that won Hatfield's approval. She was a real little lady and pretty as a spotted pony, he decided. And John Hardin's daughter! Hatfield had a feeling that he might well have done himself a big favor by the afternoon's work.

The sunset was flaring scarlet and gold behind the western crags and the ominous gorge to the south was brimful of purple shadows when they sighted the town of Marton on the plain below. Another ten minutes and they were clattering along the crooked main street.

The girl pulled the buckboard to a halt in front of the railroad station. Hatfield dismounted lithely and lifted her from the high seat. As he dropped her to the ground and straightened up, a hand seized him by the shoulder and flung him violently aside.

Hatfield very nearly went off his feet, but not quite. He spun around to face his attacker, a man nearly as tall and broad as himself, but much older. He had fiery black eyes, a square, beefy face and a shock of bristling gray hair.

'You danged cowhand,' he roared. 'What do you mean by putting your hands on my daughter?'

Hatfield surveyed him for an instant before replying.

'Sort of free with your own hands, aren't you, sir?' he asked mildly.

'And I'll be a sight freer with 'em if you don't trail out of here pronto!' John Hardin bawled.

'But you might not find them free,' Hatfield warned, his voice still deceptively mild.

Verna was trying desperately to get her father's attention.

'Listen, Dad,' she urged. 'Listen to me. I want to tell . . .'

Hardin brushed her aside. 'Going to hightail?' he demanded threateningly of Hatfield.

'Nope, not yet,' Hatfield replied.

With a bellow of rage, Hardin rushed. His huge fist whizzed a blow at the Ranger.

Before it had travelled six inches it was blocked. Fingers like rods of nickel steel coiled around his big wrist. He was whirled around, his arm was jammed up between his shoulder blades and he was held helpless, rising on his

10

tiptoes to relieve the agonizing strain on his muscles.

Over Hardin's shoulder, Hatfield saw three lean dark-faced men leap forward, steel flickering in their hands. But before they could take a second step they halted, in strained, grotesque positions; they were staring into the unwavering black muzzle of a long gun that somehow, they never could agree just how, had happened in Hatfield's left hand. And back of that yawning muzzle were the terrible eyes, now smoky-gray, of the man a stern old Lieutenant of the Rangers had named the Lone Wolf!

Hatfield's voice bit at them, like steel grinding on ice, 'Drop those stickers, pronto! Elevate!'

The ominous double click of the gun hammer drawn back to full cock emphasized the command. The knives tinkled to the ground. Three pairs of hands shot skyward.

Still holding the raging Hardin helpless, Hatfield spoke again. 'I don't know what this is all about, but it sure seems loco to me,' he said. He released Hardin's wrist, hurling him forward at the same instant.

Hardin reeled, staggered, spun around, still swearing. But before he could utter a coherent remark, his daughter was all over him. Hatfield was treated to an exhibition that would have done credit to old John in his best moments.

'You crazy bear!' she screamed, hammering his great breast with her tiny fists. 'Stop it, I tell you! Shut up and listen to me! This young man saved my life at the risk of his own. And this is the way you thank him! I'm ashamed of you! Of all the stupid, feather-brained old mossybacks I ever saw you're the limit. I'll . . .'

'Stop it yourself!' bellowed Hardin. 'Cool down and talk sense! How can I make anything out of your yappin', you vixen! I'd like to know where you got your dratted temper from? Not from your mother, and certain for sure not from me! What are you trying to tell me?'

Verna told him in no uncertain terms, with a few choice remarks relative to his own temper and disposition thrown in for good measure.

The fire in John Hardin's black eyes died down and he looked decidedly sheepish. Then a grin stretched his wide mouth and changed the expression of his stubborn, bad-tempered old face. He stepped forward, ignoring Hatfield's gun muzzle, and stretched out a big paw.

'Take it kind if you wouldn't bust it off at the wrist this time, son,' he said.

Quivering with silent laughter, Hatfield gravely holstered his gun and shook hands. Hardin's Mexican *vaqueros*, also looking sheepish, lowered their arms, surreptitiously picked up their fallen knives and sheathed them. Verna, her blue eyes still blazing, glared

12

in their direction. Trying to look unconcerned, and failing, they shuffled off.

'I'm grateful to you, son, plumb grateful,' Hardin said. 'She's all I've got in the world. I hope you'll overlook what just happened. I'm sort of on the prod against cowmen, with good reason.'

'I think you're on the prod against everything and everybody of late,' his daughter snapped.

'Not against you, honey, not against you,' Hardin replied quickly, his voice suddenly very gentle, 'and I won't ever hold him being a cowhand against this young feller.'

'Where you heading, son?' he asked.

'Understand there's a section hereabouts called Escondida Valley, with a town named Terligua down at the sound end of it,' Hatfield replied. 'Was aiming to make that town. Sort of chuck line riding.'

'You can cross my land, down through the valley, and cut off a lot of miles,' Hardin instantly suggested. 'Now I've a notion you could stand a square meal. Never saw a cowhand who wasn't hungry. Was figuring on eating a mite myself, and Verna's just like a cowhand, she's always hungry, too. Come on over to Mexican Pete's place. It's sort of salty at times, anything liable to bust loose, but he puts out the best chuck in town. I'll have my boys put your horse in the same stable with mine. It's too late to ride south tonight. We'll go first thing in the morning and you can stop off at my place on the way down.'

He beckoned the three young Mexicans, who had paused a little ways off. They drew near, looking somewhat askance at Hatfield. But the Lone Wolf smiled at them, and they smiled back, a trifle shyly. Hatfield liked their looks and gravely introduced them to Goldy. Whereupon the big sorrel accompanied them to the stable without objection.

'Reckon he wouldn't have gone if you hadn't okayed the boys,' Hardin commented.

'No, he wouldn't,' Hatfield replied. 'Goldy doesn't allow anybody to touch him unless I give the word, and I believe he'd kill a man who tried to hold him.'

'I've a notion he would,' Hardin agreed, 'but he's sure some horse. Can't say I ever saw a finer looking critter.'

'And next to Mr. Hatfield he's the chief reason I'm here right now instead of being at the bottom of Lost River Canyon,' Verna added with conviction. 'He overtook those runaway mules like they were standing still.'

CHAPTER TWO

Mexican Pete's Place, turbulent and crowded, was used to sensations of various sorts, but when the Hardins, father and daughter, entered the saloon with Jim Hatfield, more than one hungry patron laid down his knife and fork and stared. Some of the stares instantly became intensely calculating and not altogether friendly.

John Hardin paid no attention to the astounded expressions of diners at the adjoining table, but went on rumbling away to Hatfield and his daughter. Abruptly, however, he ceased talking and waved a cordial hand to a man who had just entered.

'There's the only cowman, 'sides from you, son, I got any use for,' he said to Hatfield. 'That's Ellis Gault, who owns the Boxed E down to the south and west of Escondida Valley, a fine big spread he came here and bought year before last. Gault is a regular feller. And he's smart and educated. Wouldn't be surprised if he's a college man. He farms some too, and grows good crops on what folks considered was desert land.'

Hatfield regarded Gault with interest. He was certainly a fine looking man, handsome in a rugged way. Six feet tall, perhaps a little more, he was broad of shoulder, deep of chest. He had clear gray eyes with a hint of humor in them, a straight nose and a firm mouth. His hair was tawny and inclined to curl. His clothes were the garb of a rancher except for his long black coat. He wore no gun that was in evidence, but a slight bulge in the well fitting coat made Hatfield inclined to think that a shoulder holster snugged beneath his right armpit which led him to believe that Gault was left-handed.

Hatfield's glance shifted to his table companions. He noted that Verna Hardin was also regarding Gault with interest, but the expression of her blue eyes were inscrutable. Hatfield couldn't blame her for looking at him. Gault was undoubtedly distinguished in appearance.

Ellis Gault crossed the room with long, easy strides and paused at the table. He bowed gracefully to Verna, spoke to Hardin in cordial tones and when he was introduced to Hatfield, shook hands with a firm and pleasant grip. He had a bluff, hearty manner that, the Lone Wolf deduced, won him friends. Hatfield also felt that Gault was the sort given to pouring oil on troubled waters, and with the ability to get along with most anybody.

'The heavy-set man at the corner table is Tate Preston, the one I was telling you has those Guernseys I figured would be good to breed into your herd, John,' he said to Hardin. 'I'd like to have you meet him, if Miss Verna and Mr. Hatfield will pardon us a minute.'

He and Hardin moved off together, Gault's bronzed hand resting on the older man's arm. He glanced over his shoulder at Verna as they left the table.

'Mr. Gault appears sort of interested in . . . in your father,' Hatfield remarked.

16

'Doubtless his interest is quixotic,' the girl replied.

'Chances are,' Hatfield agreed dryly, 'but I've a notion he won't find John Hardin any windmill.'

The girl shot him a surprised look. 'So you know your Cervantes,' she commented. 'Rather unusual reading for a chuck-line riding cowhand, isn't it?'

'Oh, a fellow loaned me the book,' Hatfield replied lightly. He did not deem it necessary to explain that the fellow who loaned him *Don Quixote* to chuckle over, especially the eccentric knight's tilting with windmills, was the dean of the famous college of engineering which he, Hatfield, had attended.

'I see,' Verna nodded. *'Magna est veritas sed rara,'* she quoted softly.

Hatfield was willing to agree with the Latin proverb that truth is mighty but exceptional, but he was not to be caught a second time. He looked blank.

'Reckon those are Spanish words I don't know,' he replied gravely and glanced to where Hardin and Gault were talking with a heavy-set, bearded individual at the corner table. Circumstances being what they were, Hatfield was interested in anybody who appeared to be an associate of John Hardin's.

Verna noted his preoccupation. Her blue eyes danced an instant, then became demurely innocent.

17

'Perhaps I did not accent the proper syllables,' she said.

'Not quite,' Hatfield agreed thoughtlessly, his gaze still on the corner table. '*Veritas* is accented on the first syllable, not the penult.'

He glanced around suddenly at a tinkle of silvery laughter from his pretty table companion. He flushed a little, then his even teeth flashed startlingly white in his bronzed face.

'Ma'am,' he chuckled, 'I'm through sparring with you. I'm getting exactly nowhere at it, fast.'

Meanwhile, a conversation that would have interested Hatfield was underway at another table, where several hard-faced, alert looking men in rangeland garb were playing poker and evidently taking little interest in the game, for their eyes were constantly roving about the crowded room.

'What did I tell you?' one observed in low tones. 'John Hardin is bringing in gun fighters, too. Look at that big hellion! Look at those eyes, and the way those irons are hung. That's a *muy malo* hombre.'

'Uh-huh, he does look bad, all right,' another player muttered, glinting a sideways glance at Hatfield. 'But one jigger shouldn't be hard to handle.'

'No, in the right way,' said the first speaker, 'but a slip's liable to be plumb fatal, and there'll be more of the same kind coming, you can bet on that.'

'Handle 'em one at a time, that's the way,' voiced another speaker. 'Take care of a few that way and others will sort of shy away from the chore, no matter how salty they are.'

'You're right about that,' agreed the first speaker. 'Now, listen—'

Heads drew together and the conversation became an almost inaudible mumble.

Hardin came lumbering across the room, pausing from time to time, Hatfield noted, to speak a word or two with the occupants of various tables. He and Gault had both tossed a word here and there during their progress to the corner.

Hardin dropped into his chair and beckoned a waiter. 'Gault is all right,' he observed after the waiter had taken their orders. 'He's having that feller Preston send me some blooded bulls that had ought to improve my stock.'

'Preston own a spread hereabouts?' Hatfield asked.

'Uh-huh,' Hardin nodded, addressing himself to his food. 'His holdings are west of Gault's. Over beyond the south mouth of the valley. He's another newcomer.'

After they finished eating, Hardin hauled out a pipe and stuffed it with tobacco.

'We're staying at the Cattleman's Hotel, across the street,' he announced. 'I'll sign you up a room for the night, son, and tomorrow we'll ride down to my place. Now don't try to

19

pay for anything. You're my guest for so long as you're of a notion to stick around. I won't have it any other way. And now if you'll sit here and have a drink or two, Verna and me will amble out and do a little shopping. She's always needing some kind of women's fixin's. We'll be back in half an hour or so. Don't mind waiting?'

'Not in the least,' Hatfield replied. 'It's an interesting place. Take your time.'

'Too darn interesting, sometimes,' Hardin grumbled. 'I've known lead to fly in here. Looks peaceful enough tonight, though. Well be seeing you soon.'

'Yes, we'll he seeing you—cowboy!' Verna added, her eyes dancing.

Hatfield watched them out the door. 'There's something under that curly hair, all right,' he chuckled. 'I've a notion she's got more brains than the old man.'

'But I don't think John Hardin is shy of gray matter,' he added thoughtfully, 'and maybe even smarter than he shows on the surface.'

He dismissed Hardin for the time being and gave some attention to his surroundings.

The room was crowded and noisy, but, as Hardin said, apparently peaceful. Everybody was eating, drinking, talking and generally having a good time. Then, without warning, trouble erupted at a nearby poker game. Voices raised in altercation, oaths were shouted, pushed-back chair legs scraped the

20

floor. Two men leaped to their feet. One whirled and ran for the swinging doors as fast as he could. The other pounded in pursuit, bellowing curses. He had a gun in his hand but was apparently afraid to use it for fear of hitting somebody else.

At the door, the first man spun on his heel, jerked a gun and fired a single shot. Then he darted through the door, his pursuer storming after him, the other poker players at his heels. An instant later a clatter of hoofs sounded outside.

The room was in a turmoil. Dance floor girls screamed. Bartenders uttered soothing yells. Everybody appeared to be shouting together. Jim Hatfield arose from the floor, where he had hurled himself the instant the man at the door turned. He sat down in a chair on the opposite side of the table and thoughtfully regarded a neat bullet hole in the back of the one he had formerly occupied.

'That was shooting!' he muttered. 'The hellion just slanted a glance at me and pulled trigger. Yes sir, that was shooting!'

A perspiring waiter came hurrying over to him. 'Blazes, feller, I thought you'd got it!' he exclaimed.

'Reckon I would have if I hadn't fallen out of my chair right then,' Hatfield replied, still regarding the bullet hole.

'Guess you were darn lucky you tripped when you tried to stand up,' agreed the waiter,

21

mopping his face with his sleeve. 'Those loco horned toads! Starting a row like that. They were just playing ten-cent limit, too.'

'Arguments start, even with low stakes,' Hatfield said. 'Well, guess you might as well bring me a drink. My nerves need a little steadying after what happened.'

'I'd think they would!' growled the waiter. But when he brought the drink the waiter, who was observant, noted that Hatfield raised the brimming glass to his lips without spilling a drop.

'Nerves!' he muttered as he shuffled off. 'That big devil ain't got a nerve in his body. Wonder if he really did fall out of that chair? Something funny about all this.'

It was a nice try, Hatfield was forced to admit. And had he not at once spotted the row at the poker table for a phony and, instantly alert for anything, had failed to catch the sideways glint of the gunman's eyes, it would have succeeded. But why? And who was the instigator? These were questions for which the Lone Wolf didn't have the answers, and wished he did.

The owner of the establishment, a pleasant-faced elderly man who, Hatfield decided, was not a Mexican, brought over another drink.

'Sorry you got a start,' he apologized. I certainly wouldn't want anything to happen to one of Mr. Hardin's friends. The crazy sidewinder! Shooting into a crowded room that way. He ought to stretch rope. I wish I knew who he was and I'd swear out a warrant for him.'

Ellis Gault and his friend Preston also came over to the table.

'See you got your baptism of fire in Marton,' the former chuckled. 'But all's well that ends well. When Hardin comes back, please tell him I'll see him in a day or two.'

With a friendly nod he left the saloon, the stolid looking Preston trudging beside him.

A few minutes later, Hardin and Verna returned. 'Thought we heard a shot up this way,' Hardin remarked. 'Didn't happen to be in here, did it?'

'Yes, a poker game difference of opinion,' Hatfield replied.

'Nothing serious. A jigger let one fly, and missed.'

'Danged loco cowhands!' Hardin growled, and apparently dismissed the subject. Verna, Hatfield noticed, was staring at the bullet hole in the back of the chair.

'You two wait for me a minute,' she said abruptly. 'I want to speak to Uncle Pete.'

'She's known him since she wore pigtails,' Hardin explained. 'He's a fine feller.'

Verna returned shortly. She said nothing, but in her blue eyes, Hatfield noted, was an expression similar to the look of terror that clouded them right after her harrowing experience on the canyon trail.

23

'What say we go to bed?' Hardin suggested. 'I'm tired.'

'Okay with me,' Hatfield agreed. 'I didn't get much sleep last night.'

'And chuck line riding style, under the stars, I reckon,' said Hardin.

'That's right,' Hatfield smiled.

'Did considerable of it myself, when I was young—and foolish,' Hardin grunted.

'You were once a cowhand, sir?' Hatfield asked curiously.

'I was,' Hardin replied shortly, and did not amplify the admission.

Hardin had some chores to look after the following morning and it was almost noon when they rode out of town. He had provided a saddle horse for Verna, leaving the buckboard for his hands to bring in.

'And if I ever catch you driving those infernal mules to Alto or any place else,' he began, 'I'll . . .'

'Split a cinch and have to get down and patch it,' his daughter finished for him.

Hardin glared at her, but evidently decided he'd get the worst of it, and subsided into incoherent rumblings. Behind his indignant back, Verna favored Hatfield with as near a grin as her pretty feminine lips could contrive.

The afternoon was pretty well along when they reached the great farmhouse overlooking Hardin's many thousands of broad acres. Hatfield was impressed by the fine condition

24

of everything and the comfort, verging on luxury, with which Hardin had surrounded himself during the course of his life.

'Not bad,' he admitted proudly when Hatfield complimented him on his holdings. 'Uh-huh, not bad for a farmhand who landed here with a horse and a mule and a little *dinero*. I've done pretty well by myself, all right. If it wasn't for those danged ranchers!' he added, his face darkening. 'Things were fine before they showed up in this section.'

They were seated in the fine big living room. Hardin glared south across his miles of fertile land, toward the unseen cattle spreads. Hatfield regarded him curiously.

'Why are you so on the prod against the cowmen, sir?' he asked.

Instead of glowering, as Hatfield surmised he would, Hardin unexpectedly chuckled. 'Son,' he said, 'it's a long story, but if you'd care to listen, I'll tell you all about it. Started a lot of years ago, before you were born.'

Smoking his cigarette and studying the old man as his voice rumbled on and on, Jim Hatfield heard the story of the dramatic and unusual life of John Hardin.

CHAPTER THREE

Talk in the Flying V Bunkhouse fell flat when young John Hardin walked in the door. The uncomfortable silence was broken only by the terse greeting of Bob Turner, the range boss. The rest of the Flying V boys remained wooden-faced. They just didn't know what to say and apparently decided it was better to say nothing.

All except Arch Rader. There was a malicious gleam in Rader's eyes. He and Hardin had never gotten along and it was easy to see that Rader was more than a little pleased by what had happened to Hardin.

While the rest of the hands busied themselves with various occupations, in which they had suddenly developed an absorbing interest, Rader leaned against a bunk and regarded John Hardin, who had sat down at the table and was staring moodily at nothing in particular.

Rader began to whistle, and at the first note Hardin flung up his head. Rader had chosen for his musical efforts a popular ballad in which was a line that ran—'There was I, waiting at the church!'

Rader's choice, though ill-advised, was singularly appropriate to the occasion. It was too much for the Flying V hands. Lips

26

twitched, eyes were studiously lowered, somebody sniggered.

John Hardin's blocky face flushed darkly red. He glared at Rader, who returned his look innocently, and went on whistling.

'Dang you, shut up!' Hardin exploded.

Rader stopped whistling, his expression one of mild surprise. 'Me?' he asked. I ain't saying nothing. I'm just whistling.'

'Then stop your danged whistling!' Hardin blared threateningly, his big hands opening and shutting.

Rader gazed at him a moment. 'Guess it's a free country,' he said and pursed his lips again.

Hardin leaped from his chair, rushed at Rader and hit him before the cowboy could get his guard up, hit him with all the pent-up rage of twenty-four hours of disappointment and humiliation behind the blow.

Rader reeled backwards, fell over a chair and crashed to the floor. He came up spitting blood and curses and dived for his bunk. The Flying V hands scattered frantically in every direction to get out of line.

John Hardin, his mind still fogged by the red mist of rage, jerked his gun. The bunkhouse rocked to the roar of the report.

Rader gave a strangled cry and whirled sideways as if hurled by a giant hand. He slumped to the floor and lay motionless, arms flung wide.

The bunkhouse was in an uproar. Men were

cursing, protesting, bawling threats. Two bent over Rader, shaking their heads.

John Hardin stood frozen with horror, the smoking gun still in his hand, his dilated eyes fixed on Rader's ghastly, pain-twisted face with blood frothing the lips and a dark stain spreading over his shirt front.

Hardin started as Bob Turner, who had always liked the big young fellow, gripped his shoulder.

'Get out of here. Get going!' Turner hissed in his ear 'Fork your bronc and ride. Ride fast and ride far. You're hanging on the doors of the penitentiary. Rader wasn't packing a gun. He's bad hurt. If he dies you'll get ten years, maybe more. This is a law abiding section.'

'He was reaching into his bunk. Everybody knows he keeps his gun there,' Hardin mumbled.

But he didn't have hold of it,' Turner countered. 'Get going, I tell you! Ten years, maybe more!'

He jerked Hardin around as he spoke and fairly flung him out of the door.

'The sheriff!' Hardin heard somebody shout as his feet hit the ground. 'Get the sheriff!'

Hardin's mind was clearing and he didn't need any more urging from the range boss. He got the rig on his horse as fast as his shaking, fumbling fingers could handle the cinches.

'Keep riding!' were Turner's last words.

Hardin rode, and as he rode at top speed

through the night he experienced a growing panic. After all, he was only nineteen and he had never shot a man before. For the moment, the cause of all his trouble was well nigh forgotten.

John Hardin was to have been married on Friday, or so he thought. On Thursday, his intended bride ran off with another cowhand. Hardin would have shot the cowhand, a reckless, handsome young devil he knew only as Judd, but he didn't know where to look for the man who had persuaded Eve Gregory to jilt him, nor for Eve, either. Both had just dropped out of sight, leaving behind only a curt and, or so Hardin thought, a jeering message for him.

Eve was red-haired and considerable of an eyeful. She was twenty-five and when Judd, who was nearly thirty came along, it was not illogical that her interest in the youthful and rather gawky Hardin should wane.

Such a development might he obvious to the disinterested observer, but not to a young man in the ardor of first love. Her brief note had been a terrific shock to Hardin. His humiliation was great. He was convinced that everybody was jeering at him. Arch Rader's malicious prodding had been the last straw, with tragic results.

And now as he rode, Hardin strained his ears to catch the hoofbeats of the posse he felt sure would be pursuing him. Over and over, keeping time with the point of his horse's irons, echoed Bob Turner's ominous words.

'Ten years, maybe more! Ten years, maybe more!'

Hardin nearly killed his horse that first night. He holed up in the brush when daylight came and the next night he took it a little easier. For nearly a week he rode, avoiding all settlements and ranchhouses, living on berries and roots and a few quail he managed to shoot. And as he rode, there birthed and grew in him an abiding hatred for all cowhands and everything that had to do with the cattle business.

He was gaunt and weak when he came to a farmhouse in a grove of cottonwoods. For miles he had been riding past growing crops. He had left the rangeland behind and had arrived in an agricultural section. He hesitated to approach the farmhouse. Finally, however, feeling he had nothing to fear, he rode boldly into the yard and dismounted.

The kindly old farmer, his motherly wife and comely young daughter received the cowboy hospitably. After he had eaten with a starving man's appetite, Hardin talked with the farmer.

'Heading for any place in particular, son?' the old man asked.

Hardin shook his head. 'I'm looking for work,' he replied.

'Sorry, but I haven't any cattle that need

30

tending, or I'd put you on,' the farmer said.

'I'm looking for work of any kind,' Hardin declared.

The farmer stroked his beard. 'I can use another hired man,' he said.

And so, John Hardin became, of all things, a farmhand.

His decision had not been altogether one of impulse. Hardin had done some quick thinking while he talked with the farmer. Was there any more unlikely place for the authorities to look for a fugitive cowhand than on a farm?

Like most range riders, John Hardin had an aversion to all things pertaining to farming. He could hardly have explained why, because he knew nothing about them.

But fate works in a mysterious and peculiar way. Gradually, to his own astonishment, John Hardin realized that he liked farming. He was descended from a long line of peasant ancestors, worthy folk who had tilled the soil from generation to generation. The skip of a couple of generations represented by adventurous pioneers was not a gap that hereditary instinct would not bridge. John Hardin discovered that there are worse occupations than tending green growing things in the lap of the Lord.

But as his liking for farming grew, in direct ratio grew his hatred for all things having to do with the range. Doubtless the shock and disillusionment of what should have been his wedding day, and the tragic aftermath, slightly unbalanced him. Instead of concentrating his vindictiveness on the man he felt had wronged him, he included everything that man tended to represent.

Hardin worked on the farm for several years, and saved his money. However, the pioneering instincts of his immediate forbears finally asserted itself and he grew restless. He quit his job, bought a horse and a pack mule and wandered south by west into the wild and desolate region that is the Texas Big Bend country. He prospected the deserts and the hills for gold, and had considerable luck. He was decidedly prosperous for a desert rat when he entered the northern mouth of the wide depression between two hill ranges that the Mexicans called Escondida (hidden) Valley.

John Hardin felt strange stirrings within himself as he gazed over the vast expanse of almost level grassland dotted with groves and thickets and watered by little streams that flashed silver in the flooding sunlight. Mile on mile the wide valley ran south by slightly west, toward the distant Rio Grande, losing itself mistily against the thin, fine line of the horizon. Hardin gazed with avid eyes, his firm mouth widening in a smile.

Suddenly he whipped out his long knife, dropped to his knees and cut deeply through the sod. He loosened a square of the stubborn grass roots and dug into the soil beneath. He chuckled with delight as he ran the rich, black earth through his fingers. Still chuckling, he moved farther down the valley, peering, estimating. Finally, where a grove of tall trees grew near the bank of a rippling stream he paused again, his smile broadening. He glanced about, nodded with satisfaction and began getting the rig off his horse, which he turned loose to graze, the pack mule beside it. Eating his simple supper beside the glowing campfire, he dreamed dreams as glowing as the bright embers over which his bucket of coffee steamed and bubbled.

The following morning his ax rang loudly against the tree trunks. Soon a small cabin took shape in the shade of the grove. John Hardin was building a home.

Hardin was shrewd and far-sighted. He wasted no time getting title to thousands of broad acres, which he bought amazingly cheap from the state. What he acquired was but a tithe of the miles of Escondida Valley, but farmers in many an eastern state would have looked upon it as a county, at least.

After paying for his land, Hardin still had plenty of money left. His next step was to secure hands to work his holdings. These he chose with care. He made a trip across the Rio Grande to the little villages beyond the gorge. He hired lithe young Mexicans who could ride and shoot as well as till the soil. He built comfortable quarters for them, paid good wages.

The rich soil of sheltered Escondida Valley produced splendid crops. The railroad that was the string of the great bow of the Big Bend was little more than thirty miles to the north. Hardin found a ready market for his grain, his alfalfa and his other produce. And so he prospered.

As the years passed, the little log cabin was replaced by a stately white farmhouse set in the shade of the wide-spreading trees. John Hardin became wealthy, and a power in the section, and beyond. He acquired extensive property in other sections and invested his money shrewdly.

The great majority of his holdings were based on farming or the products of the farm. His interest in the cattle business was restricted to a herd of carefully bred animals reserved for his use and that of his retainers, of whom there were many. That herd grew, over the years, until it achieved quite respectable proportions.

Not long after he settled in Escondida Valley, Hardin wrote to the farmer for whom he had worked. There was fine land to the north of his holdings in the valley, land easily accessible to the railroad. The result of the correspondence was that his former employer and a number of his friends pulled up stakes in the lower Panhandle and headed for the southwest. Before long quite a colony of grangers was established north of Hardin's great farm.

John Hardin was nearly sixty years of age, a bronzed, clear-eyed giant with a shock of iron-gray hair, when gold was discovered in the hills that formed the southern portal of the valley. As a result, a town sprang to life in the south mouth of Escondida Valley, a roaring boom town that brought in, along with its busy workers, a number of questionable characters. It also brought in other things.

Sitting secure and complacent in his comfortable home near the head of the valley, John Hardin paid little attention to the turbulent town that suddenly mushroomed so many miles to the south, even less to the gold strike that was its inception.

With more land than he needed, Hardin had never taken the trouble to extend his holdings down the valley. All the valley south of his line was open range.

John Hardin's hatred for cowhands and all they represented intensified as the years passed. A careful analysis of his feelings would have predicated the result that his animosity was largely a matter of habit. Hardin didn't know whether Eve Gregory was living or dead. And let it be said at once that he didn't care. He had married the daughter of the farmer for whom he worked, and had lived happily with her until her death after twenty years of marriage.

After his wife's death, all Hardin's affections centered on his daughter Verna.

Verna Hardin inherited her mother's small, slender figure, her soft brown hair and deep blue eyes. She also inherited her share of her father's blazing temper and implacable resolution. She was the only living creature that could make John Hardin do something he didn't want to. But with her Hardin found happiness and contentment.

Hardin's complacency received a rude jar when the word reached him that cows were being run into the southern portion of the valley. Doubtless his resentment would have gone no farther than grumblings and fumings had he not, some time later, discovered cattle complacently grazing in his alfalfa fields.

'Get them out of there!' he ordered his *vaqueros*.

Hardin's Mexican cowboys obeyed orders and the cows, developed stock and tractable brutes, departed with little urging, but the following morning found them right back in the alfalfa. This happened a number of times. A stand of wheat was trodden down and rendered worthless. The critters moved farther up the valley and showed no respect for property rights.

Hardin, unwilling to have any personal truck with them, sent his major-domo, Pedro Raminez, elderly and courteous, to remonstrate with the ranchers. This was a mistake. The ranchers had the cattleman's natural aversion to farmers, and, like most Border dwellers, were not particularly fond of Mexicans. They sent back short answers.

Now Hardin flew into a black rage and at once took steps to remove the offenders from the valley.

But again Hardin received a shock. He had waited too long and others had gotten the jump on him. A big eastern syndicate, scenting quick profits, had secured title to every acre of the valley south of his holdings. The syndicate bought the land as an investment and proceeded to cash in on it, selling it, at a good turnover, to cowmen they induced to come into the section.

With the gold strike and a rapidly growing town as the lure, this was not hard to do. Before Hardin realized what was happening, several spreads were in operation and more stock coming in every day.

But Hardin wasn't through yet, not by a jugful. He proceeded to do that which did not tend to endear him to the cattlemen: he fenced his land with barbed wire. He ran the wire from wall to wall of the valley, perpendicular, unclimbable cliffs to the east and to the west, shutting off the entire north end, leaving no road over which the cowmen could run their stock to Marton and the railroad.

The cattlemen took immediate steps to nullify Hardin's act. But here they found themselves up against it. A move was first made in the courts to force Hardin to allow a roadway across his land. But for many years John Hardin had had much to do with elections and appointments to office and so the judges did not look favorably on the cowmen's petition. The courts maintained that Hardin was within his rights. They pointed out that the railroad could be reached by way of the Comanche Trail through Persimmon Gap. A much longer route, true, and a hard drive, but it could be done. They ruled it was not mandatory that Hardin should permit a trail across his land solely for the convenience of his neighbors to the south.

Next, legislation on the subject was sought, but Hardin's influence extended to the state capital and the bill in question was pigeonholed in committee. The wrathful cowmen had to make the long and hard drive by way of the Comanche and Persimmon Gap. Grimly they promised a day of reckoning for the obdurate farmer. Hardin sent them word to do their darnedest. If it was trouble they were looking for, he'd fill 'em so full of it, it would run out of their ears.

There was some talk of taking him up on that, but it ended with talk. John Hardin was a cold proposition. Also, his *vaquero* farmhands were loyal to him to a man, looking upon him as a benevolent feudal lord who had always treated them with kindness and consideration.

In addition, the farmers to the north were plenty salty, too. Many of them were transplanted Virginians and Kentuckians, from the hill country, men accustomed to knocking a squirrel from the top of a hundred-foot hickory with a long rifle. The cattlemen fumed and swore and ran their trail herds through Persimmon Gap.

There were other spreads south of the valley, to the east and to the west of where the hills petered out into rolling rangeland. The owners of these outfits tried to hold aloof from the Escondida row, but were pessimistic as to their ability to do so.

And when the cattlemen began losing cows, it was not unnatural that they blamed Hardin and his farmer friends for their losses. For how in the devil could cattle be rustled out of land-locked Escondida Valley other than across Hardin's holdings and those of the farmers to the north. If Hardin and the farmers were not actually doing the widelooping, they were aiding and abetting whoever was.

Aside from the difficulty of getting the stolen stock out of the valley, the section was ideal for widelooping operations. South of the rangeland were hills, almost a tilted desert in their aridness. Little known trails ran through the hills, leading to the Rio Grande, and south of the river was a prime market for wet cows. The spreads to the east and west were also losing cattle, but foremost were the valley spreads, where heavily fleshed improved stock, tractable, easy to handle, were the rule.

The result of all the ill feeling was inevitable. Several of Hardin's Mexican hands, seeking diversion in Marton, the railroad town where the shipping herds were loaded, got into a ruckus with some cowboys from the southern spreads. One *vaquero* was killed and another seriously wounded.

But the Texas-Mexicans were of fighting stock. There was another row in Marton, and this time the punchers got decidedly the worst of it. This did not make for better feeling. The north and south of the valley became two armed camps. A genuine hell-roaring range war which bade to make the famous Lincoln County war in New Mexico look like peanuts, was in the making. And all because, forty years before, red haired Eve Gregory saw fit to jilt young John Hardin and marry another man!

CHAPTER FOUR

Such was the summary, as interpreted and correlated by Jim Hatfield, of old John Hardin's long-winded and rambling account.

That Hardin had made out a pretty good case for himself, Hatfield was forced to admit; but Hardin was doing the talking and could hardly be expected to do otherwise.

'Yes, it hit me pretty hard when it happened,' Hardin concluded. 'As I said, I was only nineteen at the time. Figured my heart was plumb busted. Wanted to crawl off into a hole and eat worms. I was plumb in love with that red-headed girl.'

'Still in love with her?' Hatfield asked casually.

Hardin stared at him. 'Tarnation, no!' he snorted. 'Don't even know what became of her and don't care. About ten years back one of the hands who worked on the Flying V when I was there came riding through this way. We got to talking about old times, by the way, Arch Rader didn't die, and he told me that Judd and Eve had a place of their own up in the north Panhandle country but were getting fed up with the blizzards and figured to move farther south, maybe to the Pecos River country over to the east of here. He didn't know whether they ever did or not. Nope, I'm not in love with Eve any more. Forgot all about her when I began sparkin' my Mary, who was Verna's mother. Mary and me were mighty happy together.'

His big face was suddenly somber and there was a wistful look in his clear eyes. But a moment later he chuckled.

'Funny,' he said, 'reckon I sort of evened up for what that Judd feller did to me. A feller was after Mary the same time I was, but she

41

turned him down and took me.'

'And I suppose he went on the prod against you,' Hatfield remarked gravely.

'Tarnation, no!' Hardin repeated. 'Reckon it hit him a mite right at the time. But a couple of months later he married Bob Persinger's oldest girl. They've got six kids of their own now and we neighbor together. He has the place just north of my holdings, the one with the brown house and red barns. Verna calls him Uncle Charley.'

Hatfield shook his head. 'I can't understand why you're still so set against cowmen,' he ventured. 'Doesn't seem to make sense.'

'Well,' Hardin admitted defensively, 'I've a notion I was sort of getting over it. Then those hellions showed up in the south of the valley and started making trouble for me. That boy who was killed in Marton I'd raised from a kid.'

'Any of the cowhands get killed?' Hatfield asked.

'Yes, two, in the second row up there,' Hardin conceded.

'Maybe somebody raised them from kids,' Hatfield remarked, gazing out the window.

Hardin shot him a quick glance, tugged his mustache, scratched his gray thatch, and apparently decided not to answer. He rather pointedly changed the subject.

'I've a notion Charley Persinger's oldest boy is sort of sweet on Verna,' he said. 'Hope she likes him. I'd like to see her happily married before I cash in my chips.'

'Not a bad notion,' Haffield agreed. 'She's a mighty sweet girl.'

'That's so, that's so, 'cept she's got a temper at times. I'm darned I know where she gets it,' Hardin replied. 'Uh-huh, I'd like to see her married to some nice farming feller. That is, unless . . .'

He broke off suddenly, stroking his mustache, and again shot Hatfield a quick glance.

'Figure to coil your twine in this section, son?' he asked.

'Hard to tell,' Hatfield replied noncommittally. 'Maybe, if I tie onto something.'

Hardin looked contemplative. 'Come back and see me after you get through down in the town,' he invited.

'I'll do that,' Hatfield promised, and meant it.

'I'll ride down to my south wire with you in the morning,' Hardin offered. 'Reckon you can make it from there on. Figure Tom Dudley won't shoot you, seeing as anybody can tell from a look you're a cowhand.'

'Who's Tom Dudley?' Hatfield asked.

'An ornery young rapscallion who grabbed off land just south of my holdings,' Hardin growled. 'Had the gall to wave to me and say hello the first time he saw me riding down that

43

way. I told him off proper.'

'What did he do?' Hatfield asked curiously.

Hardin glowered. 'The darn young squirt just grinned,' he answered in injured tones. 'Seemed to think it funny.'

Hatfield repressed a smile. After all, the John Hardins of the world could hardly be expected to perceive the humor of their doings.

'Came nigh to waving back at the young hellion, at first.' Hardin continued complainingly. 'Was almost sure for a minute he was somebody I'd known somewhere. But a second look told me I'd never seen him before. Just looked like somebody I knew somewhere or other, I reckon.'

During the afternoon and evening, Hatfield and Verna Hardin became quite friendly. They found they had a good deal in common to talk about. After his *faux pas* in Mexican Pete's restaurant, Hatfield made no pretense of being illiterate when in her presence. Several times he caught a peculiar and slightly worried expression in her big eyes, but mostly she was gay and witty, especially when old John was around.

That night, as he sat by the window in his comfortable room, smoking and trying to put together the pieces of the puzzle that confronted him, Hatfield heard a light tap on the door. He opened it to admit Verna.

She wore a fitted robe that set off the sweet

44

lines of her form, and of a color Hatfield thought matched her eyes admirably. She entered, closing the door behind her and sat down in a chair facing his. Crossing her knees and revealing considerable of a very pretty ankle, she cupped her chin in her palm and regarded him in silence for a long moment. Hatfield waited, also in silence.

'Jim,' she said at length, 'who the devil and what the devil are you, and why are you here?'

'Well,' Hatfield smiled, I told you my name, my right one, incidentally. You yourself said I'm a cowhand. And I'm figuring to tie onto a job of riding, sooner or later.'

Verna sniffed her disbelief of the whole story, with the possible exception of the name. Then she proceeded to give him a stare.

'Why,' she asked deliberately, 'did someone try to kill you the other night?'

'What makes you think somebody tried to kill me?' Hatfield evaded.

'I don't think, I know,' she answered. I saw the bullet hole in the back of your chair, and Uncle Pete—Mexican Pete, I mean, he's called that because he once owned a place in Mexico—told me all about it. He said he saw everything, but that you appeared to prefer to pass it off as an accident so he didn't argue the point. He said it was a deliberate attempt to kill you and that if you hadn't moved faster, to use his expression, than a tomcat getting off a hot skillet, you would have been killed. Who did it, and why?'

'Verna,' he replied soberly, I wish I had the answer to those questions, but I haven't.'

She was silent a moment, then, 'Jim, did somebody bring you here?'

'Nope,' Hatfield replied, with truth.

'But you plan to stay on?'

'For a while, at least,' he admitted.

She seemed to hesitate. 'And—and if I talk my father into giving you a job—it won't be hard to do—something in the nature of helping him look after the place, will you stay here?'

It was Hatfield's turn to hesitate. The proposition was attractive, for various reasons, but he felt he must look over conditions in the lower end of the valley before making any commitments. He shook his head.

'Sorry, not just now, at any rate,' he replied.

She regarded him fixedly for a moment, then sighed a little. I suppose it's for the best,' she said. 'You're the sort that causes a girl to change her made-up mind.'

'Now just what do you mean by that?' he asked.

She rose to her feet, still regarding him, her blue eyes inscrutable. Hatfield also rose.

'Another question for you to find the answer to,' she said. 'Good night, Mr. Hatfield.'

Hatfield sat down and rolled a cigarette. He felt that things were getting decidedly mixed up.

One thing, however, was unpleasantly

certain. He had not missed the black looks shot at Hardin in Marton the night before. Hardin's unreasonable hatred of the cowmen was being paid back with interest. One untoward happening and the section would explode in bloodshed and death.

Jim Hatfield knew what hate was. He had experienced the dark dregs of fury that destroys reason, stifles the good and brings evil into the ascendancy. Some years before, wideloopers had wantonly murdered his father. Jim Hatfield, just graduated from engineering college and seething with the lust to kill, had planned to ride the vengeance trail. But Captain Bill McDowell, his father's friend, had gotten hold of him in time, pointing out the dangers of the course he had charted for himself, the risk he was running of ultimately finding himself on the wrong side of the law.

Talking earnestly and shrewdly, the old Ranger Captain had persuaded him to come into the Rangers and pursue his quest with the backing of the law.

The chore of bringing his father's killers to justice had been a long and arduous one, and before it was finished, Jim Hatfield was a Ranger. He still planned to become an engineer some day and had kept up his studies with that end in view, but for a while longer, at least, he was a Ranger.

Now the Lone Wolf was legend throughout

Texas and beyond, admired and respected by honest men, hated and feared by the outlaw clan. Jim Hatfield had come to realize the futility of hate, but he did not underestimate its power for evil. Nor did he discount the strange, sometimes inexplicable things it causes men to do. John Hardin might well be an example of the fact. It seemed ridiculous that he would go in for cattle stealing, but the urge to ruin those he hated might have caused him to do so. Well, events would decide the matter one way or another. Hatfield dismissed the problem for the time being and went to sleep.

CHAPTER FIVE

Harpin had quite a few chores that needed attention the following morning, and he wanted to show Hatfield the workings of his big establishment; so it was well on in the afternoon before they were finally ready to ride south.

'Better spend another night here and get an early start in the morning,' Hardin urged.

'It'll be cooler riding at night,' Hatfield declined. 'I'm fresh and Goldy's had a good rest. Reckon I'll be ambling. I'll be seeing you again soon.'

Hardin intended taking a hand along to cut

the wire and repair it after Hatfield passed through the gap, but the Lone Wolf vetoed the suggestion.

'Isn't necessary to cut the wire,' he told old John. 'Goldy will take it.'

'It's a six-strand fence,' Hardin warned.

'Reckon it would be the same if it was an eight-strand,' Hatfield smiled. 'Goldy sprouts wings when he needs them.'

As they started out, Verna put in an appearance mounted on a spirited little black horse.

'I'm riding with you to the fence,' she announced.

'Well, if you say so, I reckon you are,' grunted her father. 'I never get anywhere telling her not to do something,' he added to Hatfield.

Verna smiled up at the tall Ranger, her blue eyes dancing, and made a face at old John's broad back.

As they rode past mile on mile of splendid crops, Hatfield's appreciation of Hardin's management and ability increased. He hated to think of the desolation that might take the place of peace and prosperity should the storm cloud lowering over the valley burst in fury.

They reached the wire, which was unusually high, and tautly stretched, the posts massive and set solidly in the ground, representative of the efficiency indicated in everything John Hardin had to do with.

Hatfield shook hands with Hardin, bared his black head to Verna.

'Be seeing you folks,' he said cheerfully and tightened his grip on the reins.

'If Tom Dudley doesn't shoot you on your way down,' Hardin grunted.

Verna cast an exasperated glance at her father. 'I don't think Jim has to worry about Tom Dudley,' she interposed tartly. I don't consider he's the sort that goes around shooting folks without provocation.'

'Lots you know about it!' growled Hardin. 'By the look of him I'd say he's got the devil's own temper. He packs two guns and the way they're slung sure doesn't look like he wears 'em for ornaments. Well, so long, son, we'll be looking for you back soon. Cut over to the west and you'll hit the old trail down the valley and won't have to pass in sight of Dudley's *casa*. It's only about five miles to the trail, and easy going. Sure your horse can take that wire without bustin' a leg or your neck? I still think you'd ought to have let me cut it.'

Hatfield nodded, and gathered up the reins. His gaze was fixed on the fence and his keen eyes noted that the wire had already been cut. Cut and joined again in a peculiar and ingenious manner. He said nothing of his discovery to his companions, but his black brows drew together till the concentration furrow was deep between them, a sure sign that the Lone Wolf was doing some hard and fast thinking. He nodded once more, and his voice rang out.

'Trail, Goldy!'

The great sorrel shot forward, soared easily over the high fence and landed on bunched hoofs without so much as jarring his rider. Hatfield waved his hand and rode on.

'Hard to say which is most out of the ordinary, the man or the horse,' Hardin observed. 'And you know, honey, that boy reminds me of somebody or other I've heard talk about, but I can't for the life of me figure just who. Anyhow, he sure ain't ordinary.'

Hatfield rode west, veering a little to the south, toward where a belt of thicket bristled up on the prairie. Occasionally he glanced over his shoulder. By the time he reached the thicket, John Hardin and his daughter were out of sight. He skirted the eastern straggle of the growth and for some distance rode parallel to the ragged fringe, keenly studying the terrain in every direction. Where a trickle of water flowed from the chaparral he turned Goldy into the growth. After forcing his way some distance into the thorny brush, he dismounted, loosened the cinches and removed the bit from Goldy's mouth.

'You go ahead and have yourself a little snack,' he told him. 'We're hanging around here till it begins to get dark. I want to give that cut wire a careful once-over.'

Stretching out comfortably on the stream

51

bank, he rolled a cigarette and smoked in leisurely fashion. Half dozing, he lay back and waited. The sun was already well down the sky and nightfall was not far off.

Finally the sun vanished behind the western wall of the valley. The sky flamed scarlet and gold, softened to primrose and mauve that faded to steely blue. Purple shadows flowed across the rangeland as the dusk sifted down from the hill tops. Hatfield rose to his feet and tightened the cinches.

'Let's go, feller,' he said, and forked the sorrel. Alert and watchful, he rode back to where he had jumped Hardin's fence. He dismounted and examined the cut wire carefully.

The strands had been severed in a clever manner, right under the barbs, so that the cuts would not be noticed by the average person riding close to the fence, unless they were actually looking for something of the kind. The cut ends had been bent to form hooks, so that the strands could be quickly and easily loosened, and just as quickly hooked together again. The arrangement was highly ingenious and only the Lone Wolf's extraordinarily keen vision and his habit of noticing all details, no matter how insignificant, had enabled him to detect the dextrous camouflage.

He examined the cut ends. They were quite rusty, proof that the cuts had been made some time before. The inner curves of the hooks were scratched and slightly dented. Evidently the gap had been used frequently. The question was, by whom and for what purpose. The logical assumption, which didn't seem to make sense, was that the wire had been let down to permit the passage of horses or cattle. Perhaps John Hardin was just a bit smoother than Hatfield had given him credit for. If cattle had passed through the opening it was obvious that they must have passed over Hardin's land and on north. Which, as Hatfield understood the situation, was just what the ranchers to the south contended.

There was another angle to consider, of course. Sometimes a man's workers get out of hand and pull things the boss wouldn't countenance if he knew about them. Hardin's *vaqueros* were a salty looking lot, and Hatfield knew that the Latin temperament is long on blood feuds. Perhaps the Mexican hands were out to do a little evening up on their own account. They doubtless resented the attitude of the cattlemen. In addition, one of their number had been killed. That would not be forgotten. Their minds, furtive with the furtiveness of their Indian blood, might conceive such a subtle revenge. To ruin the ranchers and drive them out of the valley would appeal to their predatory instincts. And ruin them they would, if able to continue the reported depredations. No outfit could stand such a steady drain on its resources. Such an event would undoubtedly give John Hardin intense satisfaction, too. As a motivating force it had to be considered, relative to both the *vaqueros* and Hardin himself.

Hatfield wished it was a little lighter so he could give the ground in the vicinity of the cut a careful going-over but the dark was deepening and the grass was heavy. He doubted if he would be able to spot hoof marks even if any existed. That would have to wait until later.

With a last glance around he mounted and rode westward, paralleling the wire till he was past the belt of thicket and then veering slightly to the south.

For a while it was very dark. A cloud wrack overhead thinned and a gibbous moon flooded the prairie with silvery light. Hatfield quickened Goldy's pace and rode on toward where the slope that walled the valley on the west rolled darkly upward toward the distant skyline. Thickets were becoming more frequent and far ahead he could make out a belt of chaparral that he reasoned must flank the trail for which he was heading.

He reached the band of growth, which was fully a half mile wide, and sent Goldy through it, slowing his gait a bit. The mesquite and other brush were fairly well spaced so that he made good progress despite the dark. Goldy eased through a final straggle and the gray ribbon of the trail lay before them. At the same instant Hatfield's ears caught a thudding of fast hoofs. Around a bend not ten yards distant to the south bulged a troop of horsemen.

'Look out!' a voice yelled.

A bellow of gunfire echoed the words. Lead stormed about Hatfield. He whirled Goldy on a dime and went for his guns. The sorrel squealed with pain and leaped high in the air as a slug burned a streak along his glossy haunch. At the same instant, Hatfield's head seemed to explode in dazzling light and fiery pain. He slumped forward, gripping the horn for support, as Goldy tore back into the brush, snorting and blowing. Through a fog of pain and rolling blackness, as thorns and branches raked his garments and lashed at his face, Hatfield dimly heard hoofbeats clattering southward. With his last failing strength, he dragged the frantic horse to a jolting halt. He twined his fingers in the coarse mane, desperately striving to stay in the hull, but his grip loosened and he lurched from the saddle and fell, to lie motionless in the dark shadow.

CHAPTER SIX

The moon had crossed the zenith and was well down the western slant of the sky when Hatfield recovered consciousness. His head seemed one vast ache, his limbs were stiff and cramped and he was shivering with cold. For long minutes his numbed mind refused to register where he was or what had happened. Then by degrees memory and realization returned. With a mighty effort of the will he managed to sit up. Instantly a deadly nausea enveloped him in shuddering waves of alternate hot and cold. Grimly he fought the retching sickness. Finally it passed somewhat and he raised his throbbing head and looked around.

Nearby, Goldy was placidly cropping grass. There was no other sign of life within the range of his vision and the night was deathly still. With trembling fingers he explored his aching head and found a slight gash in his scalp over the right temple and just above the hairline.

'Creased!' he muttered. 'Doesn't appear to have done much damage, but it hit me one devil of a lick. I've been out for hours. This won't do. I'm freezing to death.'

Summoning his strength, he got shakily to his feet and staggered to his horse. With twitching hands he got the rig off the sorrel and loosened the blanket roll from behind the saddle. He made shift to wrap himself in the blanket and pillow his head on his saddle. Almost instantly he sank into a sodden sleep.

The sun was well up in the sky when he awoke the second time, feeling much better. He was stiff and sore and his head still throbbed a trifle. Otherwise, aside from being parched with thirst and ravenously hungry, he felt fit for anything.

He recalled passing a small stream a couple of miles to the east and resolved to make for that. A long drink and a wash-up in the cool water were what he desired more than anything else. Next he'd try and locate Tom Dudley's ranchhouse, even at the risk of getting shot at again. Something to eat was imperative.

When he reached the creek, he quenched his burning thirst and washed the caked blood from his face. He smoothed his thick black hair over the slight cut and effectually concealed it. No sense in advertising what had happened. He felt sure the lead slinging bunch didn't get a good look at him.

'We sure threw a scare into them for some reason or other,' he told Goldy. 'They hightailed right back the way they came.'

Where was the hard riding troop headed for, he wondered. John Hardin's wire? Appeared likely. Where else could they go? It was beginning to look like cow lifting and such things weren't altogether one-sided in this infernal valley. The horsemen had without a doubt been greatly startled at his unexpected appearance, and men on legitimate business aren't thrown into a panic from encountering a single rider. It appeared that they had been extremely anxious that he shouldn't get a good look at them. Doubtless with that contingency in view they had refrained from following him into the chaparral. For all they knew, of course, he might find an advantageous position, hole up in the growth and finally elude the pursuit after a close enough view that would enable him to identify them later. Or so Hatfield reasoned and was inclined to believe that he was right.

He examined the bullet hole in his hat and burred the edges a little to make it look like an old tear. Then he mounted and headed south at a good pace. Soon he began passing bunches of cattle. They were heavily-fleshed improved stock. Slow, tractable creatures that were easy to handle and merely gazed placidly at the horseman. Quite different from old longhorned mossybacks always either on the run or on the prod. And the kind of beefs that brought top prices. Tom Dudley was evidently a cowman with plenty of savvy. Hatfield noted that the beasts bore a Lazy D brand with a steeple-fork ear-mark.

Another hour of riding and he sighted a small, tightly built ranchhouse near the banks of a little stream. Barns and other buildings looked well cared for. Yes, Tom Dudley was with out doubt a good cowman.

As he neared the ranchhouse, Hatfield saw a man standing on the front veranda intently watching his approach. He was a tall, lean young fellow with flaming red hair, keen and truculent blue eyes and other facial indications of a quick temper, although on the whole he was more than passably good looking. There was a gay, reckless air about him that Hatfield found interesting though a bit disquieting. He had met that kind before and knew they were usually capable of most anything, good or bad. The sort that made a first rate cavalry leader or an equally efficient leader of an outfit of a quite different sort. He had had the Tom Dudley variety forming a dependable posse behind him, or trading shots with him during the break-neck chase through the chaparral. Dudley might easily fit into either category.

Dudley seemed a bit suspicious and more than a little astonished at sight of the Ranger. He looked as if he wasn't sure his eyes were behaving.

'Where in blazes did you come from, feller, riding in from the north?' he demanded as Hatfield drew rein.

Hatfield gestured to the north. 'Last from a town up there called Marton,' he replied.

'What!' exploded the rancher. 'You mean to tell me you came across John Hardin's land wearing that rig and aren't full of buckshot?

'Haven't noticed any,' Hatfield returned.

The young man gave a whistle of amazement and shook his head unbelievingly.

'My cook, Hassayampa Jones, had 'em last week, after trying to down all the red-eye in Terligua, down at the south end of the valley,' he said. 'Hassayampa swore they were pink with fuzzy tails. I haven't had a snort for a week, but now I've got 'em. They're six-and-a-half feet tall and ride yellow horses! But light off and come in for a surrounding. If I see you eat like other folks, maybe I'll believe you're real.'

Hatfield unforked, chuckling.

'Would appear that John Hardin has something of a reputation hereabouts,' he remarked as he dropped the split reins to the ground. 'I didn't find him so bad. Spent the night at his place. Reckon you're Tom Dudley, eh? Hardin mentioned you.'

I can well imagine he did, and had plenty to say about me,' grunted the other. 'Yes, I'm Dudley and this is my place, the Lazy D. And you say you actually stayed overnight at his farmhouse? Blazes! You can't be a granger or a nester in that rig.'

'Nope, reckon I'm not,' Hatfield admitted.

Dudley helped Hatfield put up his horse and then led the way to the house.

'All the boys are down on the south range right now,' he explained. 'I had some bookkeeping chores to do and stayed in today. Come along, Hassayampa is sober this week and he's a prime cook when he isn't likkered. When he is, he sees snakes in the coffeepot and tarantulas in every skillet. If a real sidewinder ever-crawls into the kitchen, Hassayampa will fry him, sure as blazes.'

After Dudley had given instructions to the reptile-minded cook, they sat in the living room and smoked while the food was being prepared. Hatfield complimented Dudley on the appearance of his holdings.

'It's good range,' the young cowmen conceded. 'Nice climate down here. I was raised in the upper Panhandle country where you get blizzards in winter that blow down from the north pole. And in summer the dust storms are worse than the winter blizzards. I've known fellers who swore that during sand storms over west of Amarillo they saw prairie dogs two hundred feet up in the air, trying to dig out. Fact is, it was the blizzards and the sand storms that caused my dad to pull-up stakes and leave the Pandhandle. He was slowly going broke because of them. So he moved south to the Pecos River country. Good range over there, too, and the climate a hell of a sight better. He did well. A few years back, however, Dad and Mom both died—mighty close together. Hit me mighty hard. I couldn't seem to get over it, and everything I'd look at reminded me of them. Finally I couldn't take it any longer. I decided the only thing to do was to sell out and go some place else. Found a buyer without much trouble. When he learned I figured to set up someplace else, he suggested I get in touch with a syndicate that was offering land for sale over in this section. Their representative called on me and we looked over this valley. I liked the looks of things and figured I was getting a place at a bargain. Folks down at Terligua, the mining town, advised me not to buy at the upper end of the valley. They told me about Hardin and warned I'd be sure to have trouble with him. But up here is the very best grassland in the valley and I wasn't afraid of Hardin. So I bought here. But those folks down at town were right when they said I'd run into trouble here in the valley.'

'Real trouble?' Hatfield asked.

'Real trouble is right,' growled Dudley. 'First Hardin and his friends went on the prod for fair. They'd come to look on this valley as their own private runway. They pawed sand a mile high and started making things as disagreeable as possible.'

'Open range notions in reverse.' Hatfield commented. 'This time it was the farmers claimed everything in sight.'

'That's right,' agreed Dudley. 'Naturally, when our punchers and Hardin's hands got together, with the punchers already sore as blazes over that plumb devilish drive through Persimmon Gap, there were rows, with a few killings as a result. That was bad enough, but then the rustling started. Everybody is steadily losing stock. Folks down here blame Hardin and his crowd for it.'

'Wouldn't that be sort of unusual, grangers going in for widelooping?' Hatfield remarked.

'That's a chore it takes competent punchers to handle.'

'Oh, nobody says the farmers actually do the widelooping,' Dudley explained. 'But they are convinced that Hardin and his bunch brought in the rustlers and set 'em to work on the cowmen. No trouble to do it in this section. If you've got the money to pay 'em, you can hire all the cow thieves and professional gunmen you want, to steal cattle or murder somebody you don't like.'

Hatfield nodded sober agreement. What Dudley said was unpleasantly true.

'Yes, folks figure that Hardin's plan is to clean the ranchers out of the valley,' Dudley resumed, 'And if things keep going like they have been of late, he'll do it. A spread without cows isn't much good, you know.'

Hatfield was anxious to get Dudley's personal opinion of conditions. He decided to do a little subtle prodding.

'But you'll have to admit the case against Hardin is rather weak,' he pointed out. 'It's well known that the Big Bend country is notorious for rustling. Why couldn't it be an outfit operating on its own, coming into a section that all of a sudden promises fat pickings?'

Dudley looked uncomfortable and shot Hatfield a rather queer look. He seemed to hesitate, then make up his mind to something.

'Hatfield,' he said, 'I don't know why I've

63

been spilling my guts to you like I have. I'd figured on drawing you out a bit, but so far all I've done is talk and all you've done is listen. You seem to have a way of getting folks to tell you things they didn't aim to. Now I'm going to talk plain to you, and I don't want you to take wrong what I'm going to say. I feel I've got to make my position clear, and the only way I can do it is to talk plain. I gather you're a stranger in this section. Well, for all I know, you're one of Hardin's men. Riding across his land like you say you did sort of makes it look that way, you'll have to admit. But somehow I don't think you are. I don't think you're that kind. I've had experience with all kinds, and I believe I can judge people pretty well. I'll admit I hate to think of John Hardin going in for cow stealing and what will sooner or later come from it—murder. It doesn't seem to make sense that he would, but there are certain things that have got to be considered.'

He paused to roll and light a cigarette. Hatfield waited in silence.

'If only the spreads down at the mouth of the valley, where it's a lot wider, and the spreads over to the east and west of the mouth had lost cows, I'd be inclined to agree with you that there isn't much of a case against Hardin. But the spreads farther up have also lost cows, lost plenty of them. You can figure that the holdings down at the lower end of the valley are pretty much on the watch, and of course

64

that goes for those farther up. Now there are only two ways to get in and out of Escondida Valley, unless you're a lizard or got wings. That is by way of either the north or the south mouth. From one end to the other it's walled on the east and west by straight-up-and-down cliffs, up to where the steep slopes to the rimrock begin. The cliffs aren't overly high, but they're high enough. Neither cows or horses could get up 'em. So if the cows the spreads up this way have been losing don't go south, where else can they go but north? That's what's got folks convinced that they must go over Hardin's land and over the land of the farmers north of his holdings. Up there they can go in any direction and reach the Rio Grande or New Mexico. Understand?'

Hatfield nodded. He was not particularly impressed with Dudley's contention that there was no way out of the valley other than by its mouths. He had had experience with so called walled in sections and knew the almost always there are hidden trails, sometimes cleverly concealed, known to the outlaw fraternity but not to others. This could very well be the case in Escondida Valley and the simple explanation of the vanishing herds. He'd find out about that later.

'Is Hardin's wire patrolled?' he asked.

'Oh, yes, it's patrolled, all right, on his side of the wire,' Dudley replied. 'He's got plenty of hands working for him and can spare plenty to

65

watch that wire day and night. Isn't healthy to get too close to that wire, especially at night. I have tried to sort of keep a watch on things, but I can't spare the men to do it properly. You can't expect men to ride the range all day and 'tend to their chores and then keep watch all night. And I can't hire a regiment and give them quarters for themselves and their families, like Hardin does. That goes for the other spreads, too. Anyhow, as the situation stands, everybody is losing more stock than they can afford, and people are getting madder by the minute. What I'm most afraid of is that the finish will be a regular hell-raising range war with no holds barred.'

Hatfield nodded, his face bleak. John Hardin's unreasonable hatred, born in a moment of blazing anger and nurtured through the years of loneliness until it became an obsession was liable to bear bitter fruit. By his impulsive and intolerant actions, Hardin had sowed the wind with fine prospects of reaping the whirlwind as a result.

'Have you lost cows?' he suddenly asked Dudley.

'Not near so many as the others,' Dudley admitted. 'The valley is narrower up here and I'm able to keep a better watch on my stock.'

Hatfield nodded again, but did not otherwise comment.

They repaired to the dining room and Hatfield quickly decided that Dudley had not overrated old Hassayampa's culinary ability when sober. Snakes were conspicuous by their absence and the food was prime.

Hatfield decided it would be best to explain to Dudley how he was able to cross Hardin's holdings without hindrance. He knew that Dudley was puzzled over the matter and he had no desire for the rancher to be needlessly suspicious. Suspicious men don't talk. So he told him of his rescue of Verna Hardin on the canyon trail, minimizing the personal hazards involved but admitting that had it not been for his efforts the buckboard and Hardin's daughter with it would have gone into the canyon.

Dudley stared, his mouth open, his eyes slightly glazed. 'Good God!' he exclaimed. 'No wonder Hardin practically turned over the place to you. Verna is just about all the world to John Hardin. Everybody in the section knows that. And she wasn't hurt any?'

'Not at all,' Hatfield replied. 'She came through it without turning a hair. She's a fine girl.'

'So I gather,' Dudley muttered. His expression was inscrutable as he gazed at Hatfield and he was mostly silent during the rest of the meal, his thoughts apparently elsewhere.

They had finished eating and were enjoying cigarettes when a clatter of hoofs sounded outside. Dudley glanced out the window.

It's Walt Vibart, my range boss,' he remarked in surprised tones. 'What's he doin' back this time of day?'

A moment later the range boss entered the dining room. He was a lanky individual with a hatchet face dominated by cold gray eyes. Evidently a taciturn person, he acknowledged Hatfield's introduction with a grunt and a handshake.

'What brings you up here, Walt?' Dudley asked. 'Anything wrong?'

'Oh, nothing much,' replied Vibart, sitting down and drawing a clean plate in front of him. 'Nothing except we're short about a hundred head.'

CHAPTER SEVEN

Dudley stared at the range boss. 'What the devil are you talking about?' he demanded.

'That herd of improved stuff down on the southwest pasture is gone,' Vibart grunted, industriously polishing his knife on the table cloth. 'I suspected it yesterday, but I wanted to be sure. So this morning me and the boys went over the ground down there and also combed the whole north end of the Lucky Seven range. They're gone, I tell you.'

'Gone, the blazes!' Dudley declared incredulously. 'They must have just strayed farther than you looked, that's all.'

Vibart raised his cold eyes, after a judicious inspection of the knife blade.

'Listen, Boss,' he said, 'those cows weren't the straying kind. They hadn't left that pasture all summer. That sort of stuff doesn't maverick around like longhorns, and you know it. Those cows were as tame as cats and they were heavy and fat.

'I tell you they didn't stray. They were driven off, and that's all there is to it.'

Dudley swore explosively and shouted for the cook.

'Bring Walt something to eat,' he ordered, 'then we'll ride down there. Looks like this business of seeing things that aren't is catching.'

The imperturbable range boss ate in leisurely fashion, while Dudley chafed with impatience. Finally he wiped his mouth and reached for the makin's.

'Let's go,' he said, rolling his cigarette as he rose to his feet.

'Want to come along, Hatfield?' Dudley invited. 'Don't be worried about Watt here. He may be plumb loco, but I figure he won't get violent.'

'Might as well,' Hatfield accepted, 'it's on my way to town.'

They headed south by west at a fast pace. Less than an hour later, Walt Vibart pulled up where a little stream widened to form a considerable shallow pool.

'Here's where those critters hung out all summer,' he said. 'I keep a close watch on all the prime breeding stuff and I know. When they weren't eating you could always find them standing in that waterhole.'

Hatfield gazed about. Abruptly he dropped from his saddle and began examining the ground with a carping gaze. He straightened up and addressed Vibart.

'You say you were down here yesterday. When before that?'

'About a week ago,' Vibart replied.

'Any of your hands been here since?'

Vibart shook his head.

'When did it rain last?' Hatfield asked.

'Last of the week,' Vibart answered.

'Well,' Hatfield said, 'horses, quite a few of them, were here since the rain. About three days back, I'd say.'

'How in blazes do you figure that?' demanded Dudley.

'Look at these prints,' Hatfield said, pointing to the ground. 'Anybody can see they weren't made yesterday, but at least two or three days before. It is also easy to see that they were made since the rain last week, which, according to what you said, was five days back.'

'How can you tell?' asked Vibart.

'Look at the edges,' Hatfield explained. 'The marks left by the irons are clean-edged and sharp, not sloughed off as they would be had they been made before the rain. And note the broken grass blades. They are just beginning to turn brown—still some sap left in the ends. Had they been broken last week, the ends would be withered and dry. If they had been broken before the rain, they would be mottled with black.'

Dudley let out an astounded whistle. 'Feller, what sort of eyes have you got, anyhow?' he marvelled—'I can see it plain, now, after you've pointed it out, but I sure wouldn't have noticed it myself.'

'Me, neither,' admitted the taciturn Vibart. 'Feller's right, Boss. I told you those cows were run off. Believe me now?'

Dudley swore viciously and glared about.

'Suppose we try and see what direction they took,' suggested Hatfield. 'Those prints shouldn't be hard to follow.'

'Not for you, I reckon,' grumbled Dudley, swinging back into his hull. I wouldn't want to try it.'

With Goldy ambling along sedately behind him, Hatfield ranged about, eyeing the ground.

'Here they are,' he exclaimed a little. later. 'Headed west, with the cows in front of them. Guess you fellows can see that, can't you?'

Dudley and Vibart admitted they could, after it was pointed out to them. Hatfield mounted and they followed the practically invisible tracks at a slow pace, Dudley fuming and swearing, Vibart in laconic silence, a cigarette dangling from his lower lip.

For more than a mile they paced across the rangeland, with the long slope of the valley west wall drawing nearer. The fairly gentle slope, Hatfield noted, was based by a perpendicular cliff of varying height. Close to the base of the cliff ran a well-traveled trail. Into this the tracks left by the cattle and the rustlers led.

Hatfield pulled up in the shadow of the cliff, and shook his head. 'No following them with any degree of certainty along the trail,' he said. 'Ground's all beaten up by horses and cows. No telling one print from another.'

'But the question is, how did they get out of the valley?' Dudley said.

'You're sure there's no place they could turn off and go up the sag?'

Dudley shook his head decidedly. 'Not a place,' he declared. 'As I told you before, this cliff wall runs from almost end to end of the valley, clean to the mouth to the south of here, and better than half the way above where John Hardin's holdings begin. You'll notice it's about twenty-five feet high here. That's about as low as it ever gets. Some places it's fifty. The same on the east side. Cows would need wings to get up it.'

Hatfield nodded. He rode out on the prairie a short distance and gazed at the beetling crest of the cliff and the swelling slope beyond. On the crest grew occasional trees and patches of thicket that continued up the slope to the skyline. Well versed in geology and petrology, the science of rocks, he was forming an interesting conclusion relative to this walled valley, but which had nothing to do with the mystery of the vanished cattle. His glance roved about, seeking landmarks by which he could definitely place the spot where the cattle took the trail, in case he should want to locate it again.

Jutting up from the eastern hills, misty with distance across the wide valley, he marked a towering spire of naked rock glittering in the sunlight. Turning west, he saw, crowning the nearer hills, a rounded knob of stone rising above the level of the surrounding hill tops. By keeping the two crags directly in line, a rider would arrive at the particular location where he now sat his horse. He nodded with satisfaction and dismissed the matter from his mind, to be recalled in case of need.

'Tarnations! They couldn't run them down the valley and out the other end,' Torn Dudley was saying in the manner of a man who argues with himself. 'They'd have to pass ranchhouses down there, if they kept to the trail, and the way things are hereabouts of late, let a herd go rumbling past at night and folks would be out to look 'em over quicker 'n a cat can lick its paw!'

'They could have gone north,' Vibart

remarked pointedly, his gaze heavy on his employer's face.

Tom Dudley flushed, and he did not reply to Vibart's remark.

Hatfield's eyes were thoughtful. He sensed an undercurrent here, something evidently not to be discussed in the presence of a stranger, as Dudley abruptly changed the topic of conversation.

'You say you figure they passed here at least three nights ago, Hatfield?' he asked. 'Well, then there's no sense in trying to run them down. They're across the Rio Grande by now. We might as well head back for the ranchhouse.'

'And I think I'll amble on down to town,' Hatfield decided.

'Figure to stick around there a spell?' Dudley asked.

'For a while, anyhow,' Hatfield replied.

'Fine!' said the rancher. 'I'll be there myself tomorrow. I'd like to see you then.'

'Okay,' Hatfield nodded. 'We'll get together then. Be seeing you, and you, too, Vibart.'

With a wave of his hand he headed south along the trail. Dudley and Vibart struck off across the rangeland.

As he rode, Hatfield narrowly scanned the surface of the trail. 'I can't say absolutely for sure,' he told Goldy at length, 'but I've a mighty good notion those cows never went south along this track. No signs of it, and there

74

should be some, even though the trail is cut up. Horse, this just doesn't make sense, but it's funny, mighty funny!'

With a shake of his head he rode on, thinking deeply. A few miles farther on his abstraction was broken by a drumming of hoofs. Some distance to the left and somewhat in front, he perceived a ranchhouse set on a knoll. From the direction of the ranchhouse five men were riding at a fast pace. As Hatfield watched their approach, they gained the trail a couple of hundred yards ahead of him, reined in and sat in attitudes of waiting, their horses completely blocking the track.

Hatfield slowed Goldy and rode on, watchful and alert. He was some thirty feet distant from the silent group when the foremost, a bulky, heavy-set man with suspicious eyes and an aggressive manner broke the silence.

'That'll be far enough,' he shouted. 'Pull up!'

Hatfield obeyed the injunction and sat eyeing the other in silence.

'Where'd you come from?' the big man demanded.

'Marton,' Hatfield replied quietly.

'You mean to say you rode down the valley from Marton?' the other asked incredulously.

'Well,' Hatfield drawled, 'I sure didn't fly.'

'Don't get lippy,' the other man growled. 'Then you must have come across John

75

Hardin's land.'

'That's right,' Hatfield admitted.

The suspicion in the speaker's eyes intensified.

'Mighty funny,' he rumbled, 'almighty funny. Hardin ain't got much use for cowhands—sure don't let 'em make a runway of his holdings. But he let you across, eh? Mighty funny.'

'Not necessarily,' Hatfield answered. 'I'm a stranger in this section.'

'Yeah, we can see that,' said the other.

'Well, if you've heard everything and seen everything you want to, suppose you pull out of the way,' Hatfield suggested. 'You're sort of tying things up.'

But the other did not react favorably to the suggestion. 'Where you figure to be going?' he demanded truculently.

'I figure to ride to a town I've been told is down to the south. Terligua, I believe it's called,' Hatfield made answer.

'First you're riding up to the ranchhouse with us and have a little talk with the Boss,' the other stated flatly.

Hatfield shook his head. 'Nope,' he replied cheerfully. 'Haven't time at the moment. See, him later, perhaps. Right now I'm riding to town.'

'You're riding nowhere, except with us,' barked the big man. His hand dropped threateningly to his holster.

Dropped—and stayed there, rigid. He was looking into the rock-steady muzzles of two long guns that yawned hungrily at him.

Hatfield's voice rang out, 'Keep your hands away from those irons! What's the big notion, trying to hold up folks on an open trail? You must be looking for a chore of making hair bridles for the state. Now get back the way you came! Pronto!'

The gun muzzles jutted forward as he spoke, in a manner that was not to be misinterpreted. The cowboys turned their horses, slowly, careful to make no move that might be misunderstood.

The big's man's face was black with rage.

'You—you can't get away with this,' he mouthed thickly. 'We'll be looking for you.'

'Look careful or you may not like what you find,' Hatfield advised. 'Get going, I said!'

The group quickened their horses. Hatfield gestured slightly with his left-hand Colt, to the heavy Winchester snugged in the saddle boot beneath his left thigh.

'That saddle gun carries a long ways, and it's got a hair trigger,' he remarked significantly.

The wrathful punchers understood perfectly. Backs stiff as ramrods, eyes to the front, they rode on, still very careful how they moved their hands.

Hatfield watched them till they were small in the distance. Then he rode swiftly down the trail, vigilantly scanning the terrain ahead.

'Nice section, all right,' he remarked to Goldy. 'Might as well be sitting alongside a jury with the district attorney pounding the table. Keeps a man tripping over his spurs answering questions. Wonder where we'll run into the next bunch of inquiring gents?'

However, though he twice sighted ranchhouses during his ride down the valley, he was not molested again.

CHAPTER EIGHT

The sun sank behind the western crags and half of the valley became quite dark, till shadows seemed to rush forward over the eastern surface, and that, too, was swallowed up in gloom. But not for long. A moon soared up in the east, red and ominous at first, as if washed in blood. It paled, however, as it climbed the long slant of the sky and the valley was brimmed with silvery light.

Finally Hatfield reached the south portal of the valley. He rode on and saw on his right, apparently hanging in midair, a cluster of yellow stars that he knew must be the lights of Terligua. Straight ahead stretched a wide and arid depression, a shallow continuation of the walled valley. Hatfield's estimate of the peculiar geological formation that was Escondida Valley was confirmed.

The valley had once been the bed of a river, ages and ages ago. The low cliffs that hemmed it in were the river banks back in the old days. Doubtless the slopes were once mountain walls that eroded down to their present condition. The river ran south to what is now the Rio Grande, but was then a great inland sea. The depression running on to the south was an arm of the sea, the arid soil now doubtless heavily impregnated with salt.

Beyond the mouth of the valley proper the trail turned sharply to the left and wound up a steep slope to reach the town built on the higher ground.

As Goldy climbed the slope, Hatfield could hear the pound and rumbling of stamp mills working a night shift. Evidently the mines in the hills were excellent producers.

Terligua proved to be a typical cow and mine town. Shacks and false fronts lined the main street, with occasional more substantial buildings boasting two stories, their ground floors almost invariably housing a saloon, eating house or general store. Scattered about over the level ground were the flimsy dwellings of the miners and stamp mill workers. Long lines of hitchracks stood beside the board sidewalks, and at these a number of cow ponies were tethered. Street lighting was provided by lanterns hung on poles at the corners, aided and abetted by bars of radiance streaming through open windows or over the tops of swinging doors.

There were plenty of people on the street. Cowhands in overalls and chaps rubbed shoulders with miners in corduroys and red or blue woollen shirts. There was a sprinkling of shopkeepers and other town folk in store clothes. Here and there the long black coat of a dealer at one of the games lent a somber note. All in all, Terligua gave the appearance of being plenty lively.

Hatfield's first thought was of food and shelter for his horse. A swinging signboard turned him into an alley. The stable keeper, a former cowhand too stove up for range work, looked reliable and the accommodations offered were ample for Goldy's needs.

'I got a room upstairs over the stalls, next to the one I sleep in. Nobody's using it now,' the keeper replied to Hatfield's query concerning accommodations for himself. 'I'll let you have a key you can use to come in with. Don't always hand 'em out, but you look reliable. Feller that isn't couldn't own a horse like that. Go up the alley to the next street and turn left and you'll find an eating house half a dozen doors down that serves good chuck. I eat there. Right next door is the Montezuma Saloon, where they run straight games and pour good likker, if you're inclined to a whirl at the pasteboards or a snort or two.

'Does Hassayampa Jones of the Lazy D drink there?' Hatfield asked gravely.

'Golly yes, how'd you guess it?' wondered the stablekeeper.

'He says there are snakes in the bottles,' Hatfield replied, even more gravely.

'No, that's wrong,' the keeper answered without batting an eyelash. 'They just hand out a free snake with every third drink. Hassayampa packed home a whole saddle pouch full last week. Good snakes. Nice pink ones.'

'With fuzzy tails,' Hatfield completed the description.

'I've a notion he was lying,' said the other, shaking his head disapprovingly. 'Montezuma snakes are all rat-tailed. Well, so long. Your cayuse will be here waiting for you when you show up. I got a double-barrelled shotgun that says it's so.'

'And Goldy has some real nice teeth and four hoofs that say it's so, too,' Hatfield added.

The keeper chuckled creakily. 'He looks it,' he conceded. 'Well, I'm going to bed. Take it easy when you come in, I don't like to get woke up.'

Hatfield left the stable chuckling, satisfied that Goldy was in good hands. He located the eating house without trouble and enjoyed a satisfying meal.

After smoking a cigarette, he dropped in next door for a look at Hassayampa's snake nest. The Montezuma appeared to be doing a business that would have been a credit to its royal namesake, but no reptiles were apparent, at least none of the legless variety. In fact, the patrons appeared to be chiefly made up of miners and cowhands, about equally divided, although Hatfield noted a few gentlemen garbed in rangeland clothes that were not so easy to catalogue.

It was logical to assume that quite a few riders from over in the west Big Bend country and from below the Mexican Border would be drawn to the mining town. It was rather conveniently located for questionable characters, with the Chisos Mountains and the Border and other hole-in-the-wall country not far off.

Glancing about he suddenly spotted two familiar faces at a nearby table. One was big jovial Ellis Gault, owner of the Boxed E spread to the west of the valley, the other Tate Preston, whose holdings John Hardin had said were on the west of Gault's.

Gault met Hatfield's gaze and waved a greeting. He did not come over to the bar, however, and a few minutes later he and Preston left the saloon, nodding cordially to Hatfield as they departed.

As Hatfield sipped his drink he noticed that he was an object of attention for several of the groups of cowhands and others drinking together. Eyes slanted sideways in his direction. Perhaps it was but the natural

82

curiosity about a stranger in a troubled section. But he could not help but wonder if word of his association with John Hardin had gotten down from Marton. Finally he dismissed the matter with a shrug of his wide shoulders. Chances were he'd find out soon enough, one way or another. A little later he left the saloon and headed for bed, feeling he'd be in better shape to tackle the problems confronting him after a good night's rest. He had little enough the night before.

It was late and the crowds on the street had thinned considerably. The street onto which the alley opened was deserted. The alley mouth was dark and silent. He turned into it and approached the stable with quick light steps, his feet making no sound on the soft ground. Fumbling, he got the key from his pocket and reached it toward the lock. Then abruptly his hand paused in mid-air. The stable door stood open a few inches. He was positive he had turned the key in the lock when he left in search of his supper.

Of course the old stablekeeper might have gone out on an errand, but it was unlikely that he would have left the door unlocked and open. Hatfield recalled that as the door was shoved completely shut, the unoiled hinges let out an ungodly screech. Anybody who happened to know that and didn't wish to attract attention would leave the door ajar.

Hatfield hesitated, staring at the narrow bar

of blackness between the door and the jamb. He could hear no sound other than the occasional impatient stamp of a horse's hoofs; but the Lone Wolf had had unpleasant experiences in the past with doors that were not just as they should be. He hesitated to widen the opening. He would be outlined against the lighter outer dark, while anybody inside would be swathed with blackness. Then suddenly he remembered something else. When he left the stable, a little bracket lamp, turned low, burned at the head of the stairs leading to the rooms above the stalls. Right now there was no light inside the stable. Somebody had undoubtedly blown out the lamp. Certainly not the stablekeeper who had left it burning for his guest's convenience. Things didn't look right.

Suddenly Hatfield acted. He stepped a little to one side, grasped the knob and flung the door violently open. It banged against the board wall, making a prodigious racket in the silence.

From the dark interior boomed an echo to the slam. A lance of fire gushed through the opening. A bullet screeched past and thudded into the wall of the opposite building. Again the unseen gun cracked and a slug fanned Hatfield's face. He jerked his own gun from its sheath and fired two quick shots into the stable. There was a clatter of something falling, a yelp of pain and through the open

84

door a man charged, his head bent low.

That bent head caught Hatfield squarely in the midriff and bowled him over like a tenpin. He hit the ground with a thud, all the wind knocked from his lungs. His attacker darted down the alley.

Gasping for breath, Hatfield rolled over and fired blindly again and again. Between the boom of the reports he could hear flying steps pattering away in the distance. He sent a last bullet whining in pursuit of the sound, scrambled to his feet, still nearly bent double, and drew his other gun. Gasping and panting, he tried to line sights at a shadow flickering down the alley, but even as his finger tightened on the trigger, the fleeing shadow whisked under the street lantern at the far end of the alley, swerved sideways and vanished. Hatfield, in no shape for pursuit, sagged against the stable wall and tried to pump some air into his agonized lungs.

A light glowed inside the stable, accompanied by a storm of curses and a thudding of bare feet. A lamp in one hand, a cocked double-barrel ten-gauge in the other, the old stablekeeper came pounding down the stairs.

'What the devil's going on here?' he bawled, waving the shotgun, which was at full cock.

Hatfield ducked out of range. 'Hold it!' he called. 'Everything's under control, I hope.'

The keeper raised the lamp and peered.

'Oh, it's you!' he snorted. 'What the devil's the notion of creating such a disturbance? Thought I told you to come in quiet! You're worse than Hassyimpa Jones when he's got 'em. What in blazes is going on here?'

'I don't know for sure,' Hatfield replied, still breathing with difficulty. 'There was somebody inside the stable when I started in. He threw lead at me, came charging out and knocked me over the head. He hightailed down the alley and out the other end before I could line sights with him. I was a bit shaky.' Feel like I'm caved in around the middle. And the slugs he threw at me came mighty close.'

'Did you throw some back at him?' asked the keeper, peering about.

'Yes,' Hatfield answered. 'Let me have that lamp a minute.' He took the lamp and searched the floor, A moment later he picked up a heavy revolver with one butt plate knocked off. On the floor were a few blood spots.

'Thought so, from the way he yelped,' Hatfield said. 'Got his gun hand. Not bad though, I guess. Not much blood, and it sure didn't slow him up.'

The stablekeeper began anxiously inspecting the stalls. 'After the horses, I reckon,' he growled. I got some mighty valuable critters in here tonight. There's Ellis Gault's moros, and Tare Preston's big roan, beside that sorrel of yours, which tops 'em all.

Everything 'pears okay, though. None of 'em been bothered. How in blazes did the danged wind spider get in? You didn't leave the door unlocked, did you?'

'Definitely not,' Hatfield replied. 'It was standing open a bit when I got here. Didn't look just right and I jerked it open before starting to walk in. Suppose you've handed keys out before, haven't you? Well, it wouldn't be hard for somebody to make a duplicate. All you'd need is a file and a strip of metal.'

'Reckon that's so,' agreed the keeper. 'I'll change the lock tomorrow. Shut the door and lock it before some loafers come around asking questions. I want to get some sleep. You're all right, ain't you?'

'Fine, now I've got my wind back,' Hatfield admitted. 'I'm ready for bed, too.'

Hatfield did not argue with the keeper about his assumption that the midnight marauder was a horse thief, but personally he did not think so. The man had been holed up in the stable waiting for somebody, doubtless himself. It would appear that word got around fast in the section, and that somebody acted fast, too. Within forty-eight hours, two attempts against his life had been made. He wondered if his encounter with the mysterious horsemen could be the basis for the latest attack. Perhaps they had gotten a better look at him than he thought and were uneasy because he might have gotten a good look at them. It was not beyond the realm of possibility.

All in all, a state of affairs not tending to promote tranquillity of mind and body, but after cleaning and oiling his guns, the Lone Wolf went to bed and slept soundly.

The bed proved to be comfortable and the little room quiet. Hatfield slept rather late. About mid-morning he repaired to the nearby restaurant for breakfast. He was enjoying a leisurely meal when a big, burly man entered and glanced around as if in search of someone. Hatfield recognized him as the leader of the five cowhands who accosted him on the trail from Tom Dudley's place the day before.

The big fellow spotted Hatfield and came lumbering over to his table. 'Told you I'd be looking for you, feller,' he said.

CHAPTER NINE

The big fellow's thick lips split in a grin as he spoke revealing strong, crooked, very white teeth.

'Well, here I am,' Hatfield returned cheerfully, falling in with the other's mood.

'Was hoping I'd find you,' said the speaker. 'Fact is, that's just what I rode to town for this morning. Started early. Wanted to see you bad. I've come to eat a mite of crow over what happened on the trail yesterday. My name is Lawson, Sam Lawson. I'm range boss for the Lucky Seven spread.'

'Take a load off your feet, Lawson,' Hatfield invited cordially. 'Pull up a chair and have something to eat. A man can always talk better when he's got a full plate in front of him.'

'Much obliged,' accepted Lawson, dropping into a chair that creaked under his weight. 'Reckon I can stand a small helpin'. Came away with nothing but coffee this morning.'

Hatfield beckoned a waiter to whom Lawson gave his order.

'Yesterday evening,' Lawson resumed the subject of his unexpected visit, 'yesterday evening Judd, our neighbor to the north, dropped in to tell us about those cows he lost.'

Hatfeld's brows drew together slightly. 'You mean Tom Dudley of the Lazy D?' he asked.

'That's right,' replied Lawson. 'We call him Judd for short. A sort of nickname for Dudley, you know. Well, when we told Judd about that run-in we had with you there on the trail, he landed on us like forty hen-hawks on a settin' quail. He's got the devil's own temper when something sets him off, and he sure don't spare us. Told us we were a bunch of loco jugheads and as short of brains as a terrapin is of feathers. He said you were a right hombre if there ever was one and that anybody with as much eyesight as an owl in the daytime could see it. He said it was a danged pity you didn't shoot all five of us as a favor to the community.

'Well, we felt mighty low after that. We know Judd is a regular jigger and anybody he stands up for must be okay. I bothered about it all night and first thing this morning I hightailed down here on the chance of finding you and explaining. Feller said he saw you eating here last night and I figured you might drop in for breakfast. Sure hope there's no hard feelings.'

'None at all,' Hatfield assured him. 'From what I've been hearing of how things are in this section, I can understand folks being a bit jumpy.'

'Yes, they sure are,' Lawson nodded. 'And especially toward strangers. And when one corries riding down from the upper valley, where old John Hardin and his bunch hangs out, well . . .'

'I understand,' Hatfield smiled. 'Have you folks lost cows, too?'

'Four or five hundred,' Lawson growled. 'All prime beefs, too. Everybody hereabouts goes in for improved stock. No longhorns in this section. Why, old man Hartsook of the Quarter-Circle put iron shoes on the hoofs of his prize bulls when he drove them over from the Nueces country, to keep them from getting stove up on the rough ground.'

Hatfield nodded. 'Colonel Goodnight up in the Panhandle used to do that, or so I was told,' he remarked.

'Uh-huh,' Jackson agreed. 'Come to think of it, I believe Hartsook originally came from the Panhandle country. Quite a few of the folks down here did. That's where Tom Dudley was raised, before his folks moved down to the Pecos River country, and I've heard that's where John Hardin came from.'

Hatfield nodded again, his eyes thoughtful.

'Any notion how your cows got out of the valley?' he asked casually.

Lawson shrugged his heavy shoulders. 'Might as well talk plain,' he said. 'Quite a few folks will tell you they went north across Hardin's land,' he replied. 'But if they did, it was sure 'a slick bit of rustling. Judd's hands keep a watch over the north end of his spread, next to Hardin's wire, and they've never seen a thing. Jasper Lake of the Tree L and other folks watch the south end of the valley, and they ain't never seen anything, either. Of course it's sort of wide down here, which would give the hellions a better chance to slide through beefs they've grabbed down at this end, but how in blazes would they run stuff from Judd's holdings and from ours over four more spreads down this way without getting caught? Doesn't make sense. And as I said, if they go north they have to cross Judd's land, the narrowest part of the valley. You'd think he'd be sure to spot 'em some time. Of course, there's one thing in their favor, they never try to run off a big herd, except from the spreads outside the valley. Ellis Gault lost one herd of nearly five hundred, and Hartsock lost a passel at one time, but in the valley it's never anything like that. Thirty, fifty, now and then a hundred, always the very best stuff. And that way two or three days may go by before you even miss your cows. And as you know, that's the very worst kind of widelooping a rancher has to put up with.'

Hatfield nodded sober agreement. Lawson was right. A big herd run off now and then, with bellowing cattle, pounding hoofs, banging guns and snapping slickers, and sometimes lead traded with wrathful pursuers is spectacular, but more serious to the cattleman is a steady drain of his best stock. Such a method, if uniformly successful, can in a surprisingly short time deplete a range to the danger point.

'A smooth bunch, whoever they are,' he commented.

'You're danged right!' snorted Lawson. 'Well, here comes Judd now.'

Tom Dudley, who had just entered, glanced about and then strode across to the table.

'Howdy Hatfield,' he greeted the Ranger. 'So this loco horned toad ran you down, eh? Sam's all right, but he was behind the door when they were handing out brains. I took the fur off him and those other jugheads when I heard about what they did. They were darn lucky, is all I've got to say.'

'You can say that over twice, Judd,' grunted Lawson. I never looked at so many guns in so short a time since I went courtin' a gal over in the Nueces country and her dad and two brothers came out to meet me with double-barreled ten-gauge shotguns. Want something to eat, Judd?'

'I'll have a cup of coffee,' said Dudley, seating himself. 'Then I've got to go over to the store and attend to a couple of chores. You riding back up the valley, Sam?'

'Going to drop in next door for a couple of snorts and then I'll be riding,' replied the Lucky Seven range boss.

'I'll be seeing you tomorrow or next day, then,' Dudley announced. 'Hatfield, how'd you like to take a little ride with me? I aim to amble over to Ellis Gault's place this afternoon. Want to talk about some cows his friend Preston has for sale, some good breeding stock. Okay? All right, wait for me here. I'll grab off a sandwich before we start. Ready to go, Sam?'

Left alone in the restaurant, Hatfield thoughtfully rolled a cigarette and pondered the pranks that Fate, the greatest jokester in Creation, plays on unsuspecting mortals. He was very much of the opinion that he had just made what he considered a rather startling and perhaps momentous discovery. At first it looked like an almost bizarre case of coincidence, but subsequent reflection showed him it really was not, but a very natural development dependent on cattleland conditions as they were. And if he was right, it opened up disquieting avenues of speculation concerning the seemingly inexplicable cattle stealing going on in Escondida Valley. For Hatfield had not forgotten the cunningly concealed cut in John Hardin's wire, by which a whole panel of fence could quickly be let down to provide an opening plenty wide enough for cattle to pass through.

Could it be possible, he wondered, that John Hardin and red-haired Eve Gregory's son had gotten together? Seemed a bit fantastic, he was forced to admit, but it certainly was not impossible.

For Hatfield was convinced that Tom Dudley was no other than the son of Eve Gregory and the handsome, reckless cowhand Hardin knew only as Judd. Hardin had said that Tom Dudley reminded him strongly of someone. Perhaps the resemblance was such that Hardin recognized Dudley as the son of the woman he once loved, and perhaps still loved, although he had made a point of insisting the contrary. And, although he had led Hatfield to believe otherwise, he might have kept track of Eve and her husband, had learned that they moved south from the Panhandle and that later young Tom had come to Escondida Valley. A coalition between Tom

Dudley and Hardin would provide a perfect set-up for rustling the cattle of the other ranchers in the valley till they were crippled by their losses and forced to move out.

Didn't place Dudley in a very favorable light, but men do strange things sometimes. Eve Gregory had shown that she was strongly motivated by self interest when she callously jilted the man to whom she was engaged for another. Like mother like son? Perhaps. Tom Dudley might also be swayed only by that which tended to advance his own interests. Hatfield didn't know exactly what to think, but as a peace officer he couldn't afford to overlook any leads. 'First find the motive,' the code of the Rangers. John Hardin was motivated by dislike for cattlemen and a desire to keep the rich valley for himself and his fellow farmers. Tom Dudley might be motivated by a desire to nicely feather his own nest. And if he had such in mind and really was working with Hardin, he was in a strategic position. The other cattlemen evidently trusted him. Dudley was supposed to do his best to guard the upper end of the valley, which task was left to him. The set-up was perfect, if there was one.

During the course of his ride down the valley, Hatfield had convinced himself that there really was no way out over the cliffs. They were unbroken from far up on Hardin's holdings to the mouth of the valley. As to the east side of the valley he didn't yet know, but he proposed to find out at the earliest opportunity. And if conditions to the east proved similar to those to the west, it would appear to be a foregone conclusion that the stolen cows could only leave the valley by the north and across Hardin's holdings. And, incidentally, across Dudley's.

There was also an unpleasantly personal angle to consider. Perhaps Hardin, with much greater shrewdness than Hatfield had credited him with, had been suspicious of him from the start, might even have recognized him as a Ranger. It looked casual, but Hardin had delayed him on his ride to Terligua, and by so doing had given himself plenty of time to send word to Dudley that Hatfield was riding down the valley and would undoubtedly stop at his ranchhouse, and suggesting that it might be well to put on a little show for his benefit. Dudley had admitted that he had lost but few cows, and then on the very day of Hatfield's arrival at his place, he promptly got word that he was short a hundred head at one swoop.

Continuing his line of reasoning, Hatfield did not overlook the possibility that the trail of the herd he followed had been deliberately made. Then, upon reaching the southbound trail, where the prints left by the herd were confused by others, they could easily have been turned back onto the range. He wished he had thought of this contingency at the time.

Perhaps he would have been able to spot the point where the herd was turned back, if it was turned back. That was highly problematical, however. The valley grass, first cousin to the shorter mat-like buffalo grass of the Panhandle country, showed almost no impression of unshod hoofs.

All guesswork from start to finish, of course, even his theory that Tom Dudley was Eve Gregory's son, but with enough foundationing of known facts to make every angle worthy of consideration. Hatfield knew he had his work cut out, unravelling the tangled skein, if he managed to stay alive that long, which in itself appeared likely to be considerable of a chore.

CHAPTER TEN

Tom Dudley returned shortly, ate his sandwich and had another cup of coffee. Then he and Hatfield procured their horses and rode west out of town.

They passed the gaunt, unpainted buildings that housed the stamp mills and followed a trail that curved around the southern base of the hills. From time to time they met loaded ore wagons rumbling down winding side tracks that led to the mines. Then they veered slightly to the south and rode across the rangeland that rolled west and south to the horizon, with the blue peaks of mountains looming mistily beyond.

'We're on Gault's land now,' Dudley observed. 'Nice looking range, almost but not quite as good as in the valley, and he's got good stock. On over to the west is Tate Preston's Rafter T.'

For several miles they rode, with the dark, brush-grown slopes of the hills to the right. At times an outward flung spur ended less than a hundred yards of where the trail ran. Shadowy canyons yawned between these brush covered continuations of the main body of the hills, and once or twice Hatfield observed what appeared to be narrow trails snaking upward through the chaparral. It was perfect hole-in-the-wall country, and instinctively the Lone Wolf grew more watchful.

The ground over which they passed had a slight rise to it, a rise that appeared to end in a mesa that butted up against the hill slopes. And as they drew nearer, Hatfield made out, on the crest of the mesa, the green, tinged with gold, of growing crops. Very fine crops, he decided as they breasted the somewhat increased steepness of the sag.

Tom Dudley observed the direction of his gaze, and chuckled.

'Looks pretty, doesn't it?' he observed. 'Up there used to be dry as a bone, when Gault took over his land. He gave that mesa a once-over and 'lowed it was mighty rich soil and

98

hadn't always been dry like that with not even a blade of grass growing on it. Said all it needed to make it fine for wheat and alfalfa was water.

"And that's all Hell needs to give it a fine climate," somebody told him. Gault just grinned and kept browsing around under those cliffs up to the north of the mesa. He picked out a spot, drilled some holes and loaded in some dynamite. Blew a big hole in the cliff and I'm danged if a nice fat stream of pure water didn't come gushing out. What do you know about that?'

'There's a vast subterranean water system underlying all this part of Texas,' Hatfield replied, adding thoughtfully, 'Gault just knew where to look, that's all. A bit unusual for a cattleman.'

'Oh, he's a cattleman, all right,' Dudley replied, 'but he's got considerable better'n an average education or I'm a heap mistaken. Maybe he studied about such things.'

'Yes, maybe he did,' Hatfield agreed, still thoughtful.

A little later they rode out onto the mesa. 'And there's Gault's *casa*,' Dudley said, pointing to a commodious white ranchhouse advantageously situated in a grove of cottonwoods near the hill slope.

As they drew near, the Boxed E owner came out onto the veranda and waved a cordial greeting.

'Hello, Tom. How are you, Hatfield?' he shouted in his bluff, hearty tones. 'Glad you came along.' He descended the steps as they dismounted, shook hands and called a wrangler to look after the horses. Several cowhands lounging around the nearby bunkhouse and barn gazed at the visitors in silence.

'Come on in, come on in!' Gault invited jovially. 'Take a load off your feet while I tell the cook to fetch some coffee and cakes.'

Leaving his guests comfortably seated in the big living room, he headed for the rear of the house. There was a mumble of voices, then the opening and closing of a door. Gault came back to the living room and sat down. A few minutes later a lean, stringy man with beady eyes and a drooping mustache appeared with the refreshments.

Gault chatted pleasantly while the coffee was drunk, insisted on a second helping and more cakes, and was altogether a very charming host. After cigarettes were lighted he turned to Dudley.

'I spoke to Preston about those breed-bulls you wanted,' he told the Lazy D owner. 'He says your offer is okay. When will you send for them?'

'The boys will be over after tomorrow,' Dudley replied.

'Fine!' said Gault. I'll send a hand right away to tell him to have them ready. Then if

Hatfield would like to look over my place . . .'

With a smile and a nod he left the room. They heard him clattering down the steps.

'Ellis is mighty proud of his holdings,' Dudley chuckled. 'Always wants to show things to anybody new who comes around.'

'I've a notion he has a right to be,' Hatfield observed. 'Making a garden spot of a chunk of desert is something to be proud of.'

'That's right,' agreed Dudley. 'He's got good range, too, and is always bringing in more stock. Says he aims to grow up with the section and 'lows it's going to be just about the finest cattle country in Texas, some day.'

'How long has he been here?' Hatfield asked.

'Less than two years,' Dudley replied. 'Showed not so long after the spreads started business in the valley. Got his land mighty cheap, I understand. Preston secured his holdings a few months later. Nobody wanted the land over here, it being the longest drive to the railroad. Preston is from California, I understand. He brought good stock with him when he came. I believe Gault hails originally from the lower Rio Grande valley, Willacy county, I've heard.'

A clatter of hoofs sounded outside, dimming away westward. Gault returned to the house and a little later Hatfield was admiring the clever system of irrigation ditches that fertilized the parched earth of the mesa.

'A peculiar formation here,' Gault explained. 'Underneath a rhine of mighty rich soil is undoubtedly a layer of sponge rock. Rain water sinks right through the porous rock and keeps the top soil too dry to grow anything. But with a constant flow of water from the spring up there the soil stays moist and fertile.' He gestured to a sizeable stream that gushed out of an opening in the cliff.

After looking over the crops, they walked to the edge of the mesa and surveyed mile on mile of rangeland dotted with clumps of cattle. While at their backs loomed the dark slopes of the austere hills that seemed to frown on this unwanted invasion of their age-old privacy.

'Can't you boys stay for supper?' Gault asked.

Dudley shook his head. 'I have some chores to look after in town,' he explained. 'And I want to get back to the spread early in the morning and line up the boys to go after those bulls. If you're ready, Hatfield, we'll be riding.'

Shortly afterward they left the mesa, descended the slope and headed east.

'A nice feller, Gault,' Dudley commented, glancing back toward the ranchhouse. 'He's always ready to lend a hand and gets along with everybody, even John Hardin. He says the row here in this section is a lot of nonsense and that there's no real reason why the farmers and the cowmen can't get along. He says they need each other.'

'He's right, there,' Hatfield agreed. 'They do need one another and they might as well accept the fact that eventually they'll have to get along together. The day of the open range, as folks know it, is just about ended. Right now people are beginning to realize it, even though they won't admit it. Improved stock, fences, forage grown for winter use; that's the next order for cattleland and only the stupidly stubborn will try to fight changing conditions. The migration from the Panhandle is a clear indication of changing conditions. Most cowmen who have left the Panhandle, the Brazos and the Trinity and even the Nueces country have done so because of overcrowding, and that applies to the grangers, too.'

Dudley nodded soberly, and didn't argue the point.

They had been riding steadily as they talked, but now Hatfield fell silent. Dudley, who when they left the Boxed E ranchhouse had taken the outside of the trail, still chattered about range conditions and local affairs. Hatfield's answers were largely in monosyllables. He was constantly studying the country ahead and concentrating chiefly on the dark slopes to the north.

The Lone Wolf did not like the looks of those ominous slopes with their clefts and gorges, their slithery trails that wound through the brush for apparently no good reason. Not all of them were game tracks, Hatfield was sure. Some showed evidence of the passage of horses and possibly cattle. And what would either one be doing on that inhospitable terrain? The Lone Wolf didn't know and his interest in them increased. He concentrated on all the natural phenomena; no movement of bird or little animal escaped his attention and he followed closely any indication that his horse had become interested in something unperceived by even his alert rider.

They had covered perhaps half the distance to town and were skirting one of the brush covered granite claws that thrust out from the gloomy mass of the hills. The low lying sun flooded the long slopes with golden light in which leaves and twigs glowed and glittered. To the south were bunches of grazing cattle, but the hill slopes appeared utterly devoid of life.

It was more startling, in consequence, when a hurricane of squeals sounded on their left. A moment later, out of the brush tore a razor-spined javelina pig screeching with the senseless panic with which all pigs are afflicted at times, especially when suddenly startled. It darted across the trail like a brown streak and disappeared into a straggle of thicket a little to the south.

Dudley stared after the frantic animal in astonishment.

'Now what in blazes set that feller off so?'

104

he wondered.

But Hatfield was paying the vanished porker no mind. His eyes were searching the slope from which the javelina had darted. He saw a shifting flash of light and acted.

Dudley yelped with startled anger as Hatfield's long arm swept him from the saddle. He thudded to the dust, rolled over and came to rest beyond the slightly raised lip of the trail, all the breath knocked from his body. As he started to raise his head, Hatfield was beside him, the Winchester he had slid from the saddle boot in a marvelous coordination of movement as he dismounted was gripped in his right hand. His left slammed Dudley back to the ground, well nigh senseless from the force of the blow. Hatfield snugged beside him even as a bullet screeched through the space their bodies had occupied the instant before. The hard, metallic clang of a rifle shattered the silence and sent echoes flying from the rocks. The startled horses charged ahead a little ways and came to a halt, blowing and snorting.

CHAPTER ELEVEN

Again the unseen rifle spoke. The slug knocked dirt into Dudley's face. A third whining bullet grazed Hatfield's shoulder.

Then the Winchester in the Lone Wolf's hands boomed sullenly. Again and again he fired, his eyes, coldly gray as snow dusted ice, glancing along the sights as he shifted the muzzle, the ejection lever a blur of movement. The Winchester jerked wildly in Hatfield's hands as a slug nicked the barrel and screeched off into space. Then smoke again spurted from the rock-steady muzzle.

A clump of brush some two hundred yards up the slope was violently agitated. Something dark pitched into view, rolled over and over, jerking and twitching, and vanished from sight in the brush.

'Keep down!' Hatfield shot at the swearing Dudley. 'There may be another sidewinder up there, though I don't think so. Keep down 'til I make sure.'

He was on his feet as he spoke, slithering and ducking across the trail to dive into concealment.

No answering reports rewarded his movements. He crouched alert and watchful; eyes glued to the spot where the drygulcher had vanished. He flickered a glance over his shoulder as brush crashed behind him. Tom Dudley, still swearing, flung himself down beside him, a cocked sixgun in his hand.

'Why didn't you stay where I told you?' Hatfield reproved his rashness.

'Think I'm going to let you do all the fighting by yourself?' Dudley demanded in injured tones. 'What kind of a sheepblooded son of a moulting brush hen do you think I am, anyhow?'

Hatfield chuckled and uncocked the rifle. 'Evidently he was alone,' he remarked apropos of the drygulcher. I think he's done for from the way he flopped out of the brush, but be careful. That sort is as dangerous as a brokenback rattler so long as he has strength to fang. Come on, if you must, but take it easy.'

Silently as an Indian, Hatfield glided upward through the growth, Dudley following with less grace. The noise he made didn't particularly matter, though, Hatfield decided. He was pretty well convinced there was nothing more to fear from the drygulcher who evidently had not had a companion. His judgment was confirmed a moment later when they found the body sprawled beside a boulder.

'Know him?' Hatfield asked expectantly.

Dudley looked blank and shook his head. 'Never saw him before that I can recollect,' he replied.

Hatfield's brows drew together slightly, but he did not comment on his companion's answer.

'Ornery looking specimen,' growled Dudley.

'Typical Border outlaw scum,' the Ranger agreed. 'Mean enough to eat off the same plate with a snake. The sort that would shoot his grandmother for a snort of redeye. Let's see what he's got on him.'

The dead man's pockets turned out a number of odds and ends of no significance, and a rather large amount of money in gold and silver.

'What the devil! Here's a pair of pincers!' Dudley suddenly exclaimed.

'Wire cutters,' Hatfield corrected. 'Any wire hereabouts?'

'None except what was strung by John Hardin and the farmers up north,' Dudley replied.

Hatfield nodded. 'The sidewinder must have had something in mind, though, packing these snippers,' he commented.

Nothing more of interest was revealed. Hatfield straightened up and glanced around.

'Must have had a horse,' he remarked. 'Let's see if we can locate the critter. Brand might tell us something.'

He began quartering the ground, moving away from the body in a widening circle. Almost immediately he discovered the dead man's rifle, where it had fallen from his hands as he pitched from his perch behind a bush.

'Good iron,' he commented. 'Rather unusual calibre, though. You don't often see a thirty-thirty in this section. A long range gun and packs a hefty wallop. Interesting. Here, keep it for a souvenir. I've got the nippers. The ways things are going hereabouts, you should be packing a saddle gun when you ride around alone.'

A little later they came to a horse standing patiently in a thicket. Hatfield glanced at the brand, shook his head.

'Mexican burn,' he said. 'Regular skillet-of-snakes made with a slick iron. Means nothing up here. Nice looking cayuse. Might as well take him along with us, and you can put him in your string. By the looks of him, I've a notion he'll prove a good cutter and roper. That rig he's packing is worth hanging onto, too. You'll get something to pay for your scare, anyhow. Better turn that money over to the sheriff. Chances are mighty good that it was stolen somewhere. Perhaps the sheriff will recall a robbery where double-eagles were lifted.'

'Liable to have been the Alto stage last month,' Dudley growled. 'They got a shipment of gold coin headed for the bank at Alto. About ten thousand dollars, I believe. But say, if anybody is getting something out of this ruckus it should be you. If it hadn't been for you, I reckon I'd be a goner about now.'

'Sorry I had to dump you from your hull, but I didn't know for sure which one he was after and figured it best not to take chances.'

So Hatfield said, but in his own mind there was no doubt as to who had been the drygulcher's target. He, Hatfield, had been riding the inside of the trail, the perfect target, but he knew that Dudley, riding in line with him, would get it if he went out of the saddle and the Lazy D owner remained in his, so he risked wasting the precious second it took to slap Dudley down before he himself unloaded. He didn't want Tom Dudley killed, not just yet, anyhow, for he was very much of the mind that in some way the rancher was the key to the mystery he was trying to solve.

'But how in blazes did you spot the hellion?' Dudley wondered.

'I didn't like the way that pig was acting,' Hatfield explained. 'A javelina doesn't scoot out onto an open trail for no reason. Chances are he was asleep up there when that drygulcher holed up back of the bush. Woke up all of a sudden and found he had company. Didn't take to that sort of a snake—too big to eat—and hightailed. That set me to looking the brush over mighty careful. The sun shining right across it gave me the advantage. His rifle barrel flashed when he shifted it to line sights. We hit the ground just in time, right when he pulled trigger. Seeing he'd missed threw him off balance, that kind usually doesn't think very fast, and instead of lying low or slipping away, he kept on throwing lead at where he thought we should be. The smoke puffs showed me where he was holed up and I finally got his range.'

Dudley shook his head in wordless admiration. 'Like I said up there in the valley when you spotted those hoof prints, what kind of eyes have you got, anyway?'

'I'm just used to noticing things,' Hatfield replied.

'But what is it all about?' Dudley wanted to know. 'Why did that horned toad hole up and throw lead at us?'

'Well, looks like he didn't like one or the other of us, maybe both,' Hatfield replied dryly. 'As to just why, your guess is as good as mine. Reckon we might as well head for town, it's getting late. Bring that cayuse along.'

As they resumed their interrupted ride, Hatfield did some hard thinking, and did not relax his vigilance for an instant. The attempt on his life followed a pattern that was becoming depressingly familiar, but he felt there were a few new angles to ponder. Whoever had arranged the latest attempt, had arranged it danged skillfully, he was forced to admit. Tom Dudley had suggested the ride to Gault's place. Somebody could have been instructed to hole up and wait for them on the return trip. But if Dudley was the culprit, he had evinced a grim courage and a reckless disregard for possible personal consequences that was a bit out of the ordinary. When two men ride side by side, a rifleman several hundred yards distant has to be a mighty skillful marksman to be sure he'll plug the right one. A little wavering of his gun barrel and the other gent is likely to get it. It would certainly take iron nerve to ride along calmly under such circumstances, not knowing from one minute to the next when lead would whine through the air from a distance. All the way from the Gault ranchhouse, Dudley had certainly not evinced any apprehension or given any indications that he was under undue strain. Hatfield did not doubt that he possessed reckless courage, but courage in the face of danger is one thing, iron control over the emotions something else again. If Tom Dudley had arranged the drygulching to take place under the conditions it did, he was something to reckon with.

Of course, Hatfield had to admit, somebody watching them ride out of town and knowing they were headed for the Gault ranch would surmise that they'd come riding back, doubtless before nightfall. Which would provide ample opportunity for planting the rifleman in a strategic position. With two attempts on his life having been made in just about that number of days, it was not far-fetched to assume that somebody was waiting for an opportunity to make a third try.

He was convinced of one thing. Whoever was trying to kill him was mixed up in the cattle stealing. Somebody feared him and felt he must be liquidated at all costs and as quickly as possible. Began to look like, he ruefully admitted, somebody had recognized him, somebody familiar with the exploits of the Lone Wolf and who had guts enough to kill a Ranger.

Theory again, of course, but the known facts pointed in that direction. But be that as it might, Hatfield knew well that his life depended on his finding the right answers to the various questions, and without delay. He abruptly asked Dudley a question.

'Tom,' he said, 'about how many head of stock have been stolen in this section during the past month, would you say?'

Dudley wrinkled his brows in thought. 'Well, including what the spreads in the valley have lost and the outfits down this side of it, I'd say something between two and three thousand head.'

Hatfield whistled under his breath. That meant, with the price of 'wet' cows what it was, somebody was cleaning up better than a thousand dollars a day. No wonder the wideloopers were ready to murder rather than have their rich pickings interrupted.

Before starting back to town, Hatfield had blazed a white patch on a tree trunk to guide whoever came for the body of the dead owlhoot.

'I suppose the sheriff's office is at Marton,' he remarked to his companion. I believe that's the county seat.'

'That's right,' replied Dudley, 'but there's a deputy stationed at Terligua.'

'We'll report to him,' Hatfield decided. 'He can come out and pack the body in on the chance that somebody in town might recognize the sidewinder and tie him up with somebody. Perhaps we should have brought it in ourselves, but peace officers usually like to look a body over where the killing takes place. Reckon he'll keep till tomorrow.'

'I'll bet there isn't a coyote or buzzard in the Big Bend that would touch that poisonous reptile,' Dudley growled.

The hills were purpling with dusk as they drew near Terligua and the grumble of the stamp mills sounded loud in the evening hush.

Dudley, who had been silent for some time, suddenly asked the question, 'Tied up with anybody yet?'

Hatfield shook his head. 'Haven't had time to look around any,' he replied.

'How'd you like to sign up with me?' Dudley suggested. 'I can use another top hand or two, and I'd sure like to have you with me.'

Hatfield considered it a moment. The proposition had its attractions. He might be walking into a trap, but he felt he had to chance it. If there was any place where he would have an opportunity to learn just what was going on in Escondida Valley, he figured it was the Lazy D. Among other things, it would offer the best chance to keep an eye on John Hardin's wire.

'Okay,' he accepted briefly. 'Reckon you've hired yourself a hand.'

'And I pay better than average wages,' Dudley said. 'Hope you'll like it with us. I believe you will. The boys are a good bunch.'

Upon arriving at town, they at once looked up the deputy sheriff and acquainted him with what had happened on the trail.

The deputy, a former cowhand, swore pungently. Danged section's getting worse all the time,' he concluded. 'Nobody's safe any more. Reckon the sidewinder figured you boys had some pickings on you. Plenty in this section of late who'd kill for a couple of pesos or your horses. Okay, I'll ride out there tomorrow with a couple of fellers and a mule and pack in the body. Nope, no sense in you fellers sticking around. It'll take time to notify the coroner up at Marton. I'll let you know if he 'lows to set on the horned toad and wants your evidence. Couldn't do it before day after tomorrow at the earliest.'

'I'll be down here day after tomorrow,' Dudley said. 'The boys are going over to Tate Preston's place to pick up a bunch of cows I'm buying. I'll ride this far with them and bring Hatfield along. He's signed up with me.'

'That'll be fine,' said the deputy. 'A tree trunk marked with a blaze, eh? And the body right in line with it about two hundred yards up the slope? Should be easy to locate. Chances are there'll be a buzzard or two roosting around waiting for him to get ripe. Okay, be seeing you.'

Hatfield did not mention to the deputy the wire cutters he had taken from the dead drygulcher's pocket. Dudley appeared to have forgotten all about them. The unexpected find puzzled the Ranger and he had a feeling that it was important. Why should the fellow have been packing such a thing? Hatfield was sure that other than what John Hardin had stretched across the valley, there wasn't a strand of barbed wire within forty miles. There were no poison springs or streams in this region that needed to be fenced, and to the cowmen of the Big Bend, 'bobbed' wire, as they called it, was anathema. So what use would anybody have for such a tool, part of the cowhand's equipment in the Panhandle and other sections where there was fenced range. If it were to be used at all, it would have to be used on Hardin's fence, and what could that mean? Hatfield didn't know but he had an uneasy premonition that from his inability to read this particular enigma would come trouble.

CHAPTER TWELVE

Hatfield and Dudley had something to eat and shortly afterward went to bed and enjoyed a peaceful night. They left town at daylight the following morning and reached the Lazy D without event.

Things were different, however, when they

entered the ranchhouse. Vibart, the range boss was waiting for them, his long face more lugubrious than usual.

'Well,' he said without preamble, 'they got something better'n fifty head last night, from the southeast pasture, that herd of breeding stock.'

'What!' bawled Dudley, his face turning scarlet.

'That's what I said,' returned Vibart. 'They were there yesterday morning, this morning they weren't.'

Dudley swore a vicious oath. 'Did you try to track 'em?' he asked.

Vibart shrugged his scrawny shoulders. 'What was the use?' he asked. 'And anyhow, we ain't got Hatfield's eyes.'

Dudley swore some more. 'Well, thank God, I've got somebody at last I can depend on to do the right thing,' he concluded. 'I've signed up Hatfield. And soon as we have something to eat, we're riding to that pasture and pick up that trail.'

Vibart shrugged again and went out to the kitchen to confer with the cook.

'Why in blazes didn't he try to track them?' Dudley demanded of Hatfield. 'If this isn't the limit!'

'Don't be too hard on him,' Hatfield said. 'Remember, cowhands aren't usually trackers. It's seldom they are off a horse. You have to have some experience at that sort of thing to be much good at it.'

'I reckon,' Dudley conceded in irritated tones. 'But you're a cowhand and you seem to have the hang of it.'

'I wasn't always a cowhand,' Hatfield replied, without amplifying the statement.

'I can well imagine that, too,' Dudley agreed. 'Well, let's eat and then see what we can do. This is getting serious. At this rate it won't be long till I'm out of business. Along with everybody else in this darn valley,' he added morosely.

After eating they rode to the pasture in question, and after considerable searching, Hatfield did manage to pick up the trail.

'But I couldn't have done, it if it wasn't for one lucky thing,' he told Dudley.

'What's that?' asked the rancher.

'One of the wideloopers was riding a horse with brand-new shoes with mighty long calks,' Hatfield explained. 'They cut into the grass deeply enough to leave broken stalks close to the roots. Come here and I'll show you.'

Bending over the grass, Dudley was able to spot the evidence.

'Guess I'll have to take back what I said to Vibart,' he admitted. 'I don't believe anybody else in the valley would have noticed that. Think you can follow the tracks?'

'On foot,' Hatfield replied. 'That is if I don't go lame in these high-heeled boots. Guess I should have brought along moccasins.'

118

At first it was a slow business, but after a mile or so, Hatfield mounted his horse.

'They lead straight across the valley toward the west wall,' he said quietly. 'I've a pretty good notion they are not going to turn, and I can spot a deeper print now and then from up here.'

Hatfield was right, the tracks did lead straight across the valley to the north-south trail, where they were swallowed up in a multitude of prints. He could no longer even be sure about the deep calk marks of the horse with the new shoes.

Dudley swore in exasperation. 'Everything seems to work to the advantage of the hellions,' he fumed. 'The cows have a habit of drifting over onto the trail in the late afternoon, to chew their cuds in the shade of the cliffs. The trail's always cut all to hell by their hoofs.'

If there'd just been a rain last night, it might be different,' Hatfield remarked thoughtfully. 'Then the tracks left by driven cattle would have scored deep and might remain distinct from the others. But it didn't, so that's out.'

He hooked his leg over the horn, rolled a cigarette and lighted it, gazing absently across the valley. Then abruptly his glance remained fixed, while the forgotten cigarette burned toward his fingers. He was gazing straight at a tall, glittering spire of naked rock that fanged up from the general level of the hilltops east of the valley. He dropped his foot into the stirrup, rode out on the prairie a little ways and gazed westward. Directly in line with the distant spire, a jutting knob of stones rose from the western hill crests. The two were the landmarks he noted the day the first stolen herd was tracked to the trail.

What was the answer, he wondered. Through his mind again drifted the suspicion that the whole thing was a plant, the stories of the missing Lazy D cows so much sheep dip. Well, if that was so, he had inadvertently stumbled upon the finest bunch of actors that never trod the boards, in the persons of Tom Dudley, Vibart and the Lazy D hands.

But the suspicion persisted. He had twice tracked herds across the valley to this spot, true, but what guarantee had he that they were really Lazy D stock? They could just as well have been cows rustled from other spreads farther down the valley. But why were they both times brought to this particular spot?

He speculated on the two prominent crags. They would be clearly visible on a moonlight night, or even on a night of bright starlight, for that matter, and they would provide reliable guide posts for anybody seeking to reach this particular spot on the trail. A spot that might have been chosen for a meeting point, the point where riders coming down from the north could take over the widelooped herd. By that method whoever lifted the cows would be able to get back home, whenever the blazes that was, before daylight. The stolen herd would be on the fenced lands to the north before it was light, where the cattlemen from the south did not dare venture. The purloined beefs could be holed up somewhere in safety until it was feasible to start them on their trip to New Mexico or across the Rio Grande.

And there was the cut in John Hardin's wire. The exasperated Ranger felt sure that the cut worked into the scheme somehow. Well, he would find out about that, he promised himself grimly, if he managed to stay alive long enough.

'What say, Jim?' Dudley called. 'Shall we try and follow 'em for a while? Vibart wants to ride north.'

'You're the boss,' Hatfield replied, 'but I'm telling you there isn't a chance with the trail cut up like it is.'

'Oh, the devil with it, then!' decided Dudley. 'Vibart, you might as well get back on the job. Round up the boys and have them check everything on the southeast pastures. We might as well get a shipping herd together and sell a few before they're all gone. I can use the money right now. I'll get in touch with the Armon people. They should be willing to take a couple of hundred head in ten days or a couple of weeks. Okay, Hatfield and me'll spend the rest of the afternoon riding around and looking things over, so he'll be getting lined up on the range!'

With a grunt and a nod, the taciturn range boss turned his horse's head to the southeast and rode off swiftly. Hatfield and Dudley rode east at a more leisurely pace.

They covered a lot of ground in the course of the afternoon, Dudley pointing out matters of importance relative to the various chores to be done. Finally they reached the cliffs that walled the valley on the east. Dudley gestured to the rugged barrier.

'Like that all the way to the valley mouth, just the same as on the west,' he observed. 'See now how impossible it is to get out except by the north or the south?'

Hatfield nodded. He was inclined to believe Dudley was right. He was certain in his own mind that the valley had once been the canyon bed of a great river. That being the case, it was logical to assume that the cliff wall extended unbroken to the south mouth. He'd check on the matter later, when opportunity afforded, but had little hope now of finding a hidden way out of the valley.

It was past sunset when they got back to the ranchhouse. There they found big Sam Lawson, the Lucky Seven range boss, impatiently awaiting their arrival.

'You had your patrols out last night, Judd?' he asked after growling a greeting.

'Two men staying as close to Hardin's wire as they considered safe,' Dudley replied.

'And they didn't see anything?'

'Not a thing. What are you getting at, Sam?'

'Oh, nothing much, except we lost about fifty head last night. A bunch that was pastured almost within sight of the ranchhouse.'

Dudley swore. 'Any notion which direction they took?' he asked.

'Well, if they went south, they must have passed over Jasper Lake's holdings, where his boys were patrolling, and over the Bar S and the Donners' place, and they were patrolled, too,' Lawson replied, his voice heavy with implication.

'But you don't figure they did,' Dudrey finished for him.

'No, and neither do you,' Lawson said flatly. 'What do you think, Vibart?'

The taciturn range boss shrugged his shoulders and jerked his head in a northerly direction.

'He never changes his mind about that,' Dudley interposed. 'As for me, I don't know what the devil to think. Let me tell you what happened to Hatfield and me yesterday.'

Jackson listened in silence, his face darkening with anger, till Dudley finished his account of the attempted drygulching. Then his comments were vigorous and profane.

'There'll never be any peace in this section till every danged nester is run out,' he finished.

'The feller who threw lead at us wasn't a

farmer,' Dudley protested.

'Of course he wasn't!' Jackson snorted. 'You say you never saw him before. And I'm ready to bet a hatful of pesos right now that it'll turn out that nobody in the section ever saw him before, either. That is nobody who'll admit having seen him. Of course they didn't. He was brought in to do the chore. Trust John Hardin and his bunch to be smart enough for that. They'd hired their gunmen over in New Mexico or down south of the line. Found a hefty passel of *dinero* in his pocket, you said? Uh-huh, the money he was paid in advance to do the chore, and a bonus promised him when he brought in the scalp! Money might have come from the Alto stage robbery. How terrapin-stupid can you get! That robbery happened a month ago. Whoever heard of that sort hanging onto his stealings that long! That lousy son of a vangaroon spider got paid off plumb recent. Remember what I said, I've got money in my pocket to bet right now that when Deputy Shafter brings in the body nobody will have ever seen the hellion before. Any takers?'

The Lazy D bunch, including Dudley, looked uncomfortable and made no move to accept the wager.

'And I'll tell you something else,' Lawson went on, working himself into a rage. 'It's just a matter of time and time's getting short, till the cowmen of this section are going to ride up this valley, and there'll be a showdown. And when it's finished, the only nesters left in this valley will be good ones, and you know what that means. That's what the old-timers used to say about Apaches, the only good one was a dead one. It goes for nesters.'

Nobody seemed willing to try and answer Lawson's argument. Jim Hatfield kept his face expressionless, but he was far from expressionless inside. What Lawson said was no wild figment of the imagination of anger. It was cold truth.

'Yes, they're not satisfied with ruining us, now they're starting to kill us off,' Lawson added as he rose to go. 'You were the first try, Judd, and if it hadn't been for Hatfield being smarter than a tree full of owls, you would have been the first rancher out of the way. Wonder who the devil's marked for the next deal?'

And as the Lazy D hands exchanged furtive glances, it was easy to see that they were doing a little uncomfortable wondering, too.

Jim Hatfield went to bed in no pleasant frame of mind. For once, perhaps for the first time in the course of his Ranger career, the Lone Wolf was feeling a bit shaky. The situation might get out of hand with the suddenness of a dynamite explosion. He debated whether to ride to Marton and send a telegram to Captain Bill McDowell, urging him to dispatch a troop of Rangers to the section without delay. But to do so, Captain Bill would have to withdraw men from localities where they were badly needed. After appraising the situation with a concentration that amounted to mental agony, Hatfield decided to wait a while on the chance that something might occur that would lead him to whoever was responsible for the deplorable condition.

For there was no doubt in Hatfield's mind but that somewhere there was a mastermind directing operations. But he could draw no definite conclusion about who it could be. Somewhere there was a man of cold courage, utter ruthlessness and far more than average brain power. But who in blazes was the man? John Hardin? Hardin had proven by his accomplishments that he possessed beyond ordinary ability. Hatfield couldn't help but think that Hardin was given to direct methods. He felt that Hardin was more liable to get his *vaqueros* together and ride down the valley looking for trouble. From all he had been able to learn of the man, that would be the Hardin method of procedure. Tom Dudley? Hatfield wasn't sure. Dudley did a lot of talking and didn't say much. He also evinced alertness of mind and a capability for reckless, daring. But, as in the case of Hardin, Hatfield just couldn't see the Lazy D owner as having enough beneath his hair to plan and execute such a campaign of lawlessness as was plaguing the section.

Of course, both Hardin and Dudley might be but pawns in the hands of a more able and adroit man who was putting their emotions and ambitions to use to his own advantage. But—the question to which Hatfield had no answer—who? He didn't know, but he did know that he had to find out if he were to remain among the living, and, even more important from the Lone Wolf's point of view, prevent a range war that would drench Escondida Valley with blood, the innocent suffering with the guilty.

When Hatfield and Dudley reached Terligua the following day, shortly before noon, a surprise awaited them. Deputy Shafter was in his little office when they arrived to make report. He looked them over searchingly.

'You fellers sure you didn't dream up what you told me happened out on the west trail yesterday?' he asked.

'Well,' Hatfield smiled reply, 'if we did, we also dreamed up a horse, a rifle and that nearly two hundred dollars in gold I handed you the other night. What makes you ask?'

'Because,' the deputy said slowly, 'I followed instructions and found the blazed tree, all right, but there wasn't any corpse up there in the brush where you said it would be.'

CHAPTER THIRTEEN

Tom Dudley swore. Hatfield stared at the deputy with narrowing eyes. 'You're sure?' he asked quietly.

'I'm sure,' Shafter returned. 'We went over every inch of the ground north of that blaze on the tree trunk. Wasn't as much as a loose hair of him laying around. But we did find these.'

He drew three empty brass shells from his pocket. 'Thirty-thirties,' he said. If we hadn't found them I'd have thought maybe you fellers got mixed up on your location or something. These cartridges had been fresh shot though, and it's mighty nigh certain they came out of the rifle you packed to town the other night. Sure you didn't just crease the devil and he came to later and got away?'

'No, he wasn't creased,' Hatfield stated definitely. I looked him over. His coat was dusted on both sides, right over the heart. He didn't walk away by himself.'

'Which means somebody packed him off,' said the deputy.

'Which also means somebody was afraid he might be recognized if folks here in town got a look at him,' Hatfield added.

The deputy nodded. 'That's the way I see it,' he admitted.

'Which means also,' Hatfield said, 'that the

jigger wasn't working alone. His motive wasn't robbery or horse stealing. Somebody sent him out to do the chore and when he didn't show up they went looking for him, found what was left of him and packed it off.'

'And that means,' Dudley exclaimed excitedly, 'that somebody here in town watched us ride out, heading for Gault's place, and had that tarantula hole up and wait for us coming back.'

'Could be,' Hatfield conceded noncommittally.

Dudley was silent for some moments, apparently thinking deeply.

'Sort of knocks the props from under Sam Lawson's argument, that the farmers were responsible,' he said slowly. 'Even admitting that they brought some jigger in to do their gunning for them, it sure doesn't seem likely that they'd have a bunch down here in town directing things, does it?'

'Would be a mite out of the ordinary, to say the least,' the deputy had to admit. Hatfield said nothing.

'Well, Jim, seeing as we don't have to attend an inquest, I reckon we might as well head back to the spread,' Dudley suggested. 'We'll stop off at the Montezuma and hand the boys their powders. I told them to wait for us there.'

At the Montezuma, Dudley issued his instructions to Vibart, which the range boss received with an understanding nod.

'All right,' he said. 'We'll spend the night at Preston's place and head back with the cows first thing in the morning. We'd ought to make it to our pasture by dark tomorrow night, or a little before. Doesn't matter if we don't, though. There's a moon and it's easy going up the trail.'

'Take your time, I don't want those critters pushed,' directed Dudley. 'They're fat and heavy and it isn't good to shove 'em. And be sure you don't let some hellion lift 'em from under your nose.'

'I'd like to see 'em try it,' was Vibart's grim reply. 'If they do, we'll settle this widelooping business once and for all.'

'Preston always has some good stuff for sale,' Dudley remarked as they rode out of town. Me and Gault are always bringing in stock and buying more land. Looks like they aim to control the whole section, in time.'

'That's the way big outfits get their start,' Hatfield conceded. 'They must have considerable money to spend.'

'Seem to,' agreed Dudley. 'Of course they do a lot of shipping and their stuff brings top prices in the market. They're both yelling about their losses of late, though. Down here it's different than in the valley. When a herd is lifted it's a big one. Terwilliger over to the east lost close to five hundred head one night and even more another time. In the valley we only lose comparatively small bunches, but we lost 'em too danged often.'

'And losses of that kind eventually put the rancher out of business,' Hatfield observed. 'No outfit can stand a steady drain on its resources.'

'You're darn right,' Dudley agreed gloomily, 'and the fact that they operate steadily on a small scale is what makes it so danged hard to drop a loop on the sidewinders. No outfit has enough men to properly patrol its holdings against that kind of stealing. You can guard a big herd, but how in blazes are you going to keep an eye on little bunches scattered all over the range? And, speaking of patrols, I reckon it's up to you and me to ride tonight. We sort of take turns at the night riding. We'll have something to eat and rest up a bit and then light out. You can take the east side of the valley and I'll cover the west side. Keep an eye on Hardin's wire, but don't get too close. If you do one of those damn *vaqueros* is liable to drop a slug in your direction. They're a suspicious lot, and darn good shots. Stay back far enough to be out of range.'

Hatfield obeyed instructions to a point, he rode eastward almost to the cliffs, but when he turned back west, he proceeded well beyond the middle of the valley, almost to the cleverly concealed cut in Hardin's wire. He was riding from a thicket some eight hundred yards east of the cut when he suddenly pulled Goldy to a halt in the shadow. The moon had risen and by the silvery light he saw a horseman pacing along the wire from the west. The distance was too great to distinguish features or other identifying marks, but from the man's general build he felt pretty sure it was Tom Dudley. Sitting his horse well back in the shadow, he watched the horseman's progress.

When he was about where Hatfield estimated the cut should be, he pulled up and dismounted. Hatfield could see that he was working on the fence and surmised that he was loosening the cut strands and dropping them to the ground. A moment later he went back to his horse and swung himself into the saddle.

However, he did not ride away, but lounged in the saddle. Looked very much like he was waiting for somebody.

A few minutes later, Hatfield was sure of it. He spotted another rider coming at a swift gait from the north, across Hardin's land. The new arrival passed through the cut in the fence and pulled up alongside Dudley. Hatfield could see the two heads draw together as if in low-voiced conversation. He would have greatly liked to hear what was said, but it was impossible. He could not draw nearer over the lighted prairie.

A few minutes passed, then the pair turned their horses and rode slowly to the southwest until the shadow of a belt of thicket swallowed them.

Hatfield thought about what he should do. Under the circumstances, to ride across the moonlit range was rank nonsense. He could not hope to remain undetected if the pair happened to be keeping a lookout, as very probably they were. And the first intimation that they had spotted him might well be a slug he would feel, but not hear. There was nothing to do but stay where he was and await developments. He rolled a cigarette, carefully cupped a match in his hands so its flicker could not be seen from a distance and lighted the brain tablet. Lounging comfortably in the saddle, he smoked and waited.

Half an hour or so passed and the pair reappeared, riding slowly and dose together. At the wire they drew rein, apparently talked for a few minutes longer. Then one headed north at a fast pace. Dudley, Hatfield felt sure it was Dudley, dismounted, evidently hooked up the wire and then rode away slowly in a westward direction. Hatfield waited until he was out of sight before he rode from the shadow, thinking about what he had seen.

It was evident that Tom Dudley had met somebody from the north, doubtless a prearranged meeting. Just what did it mean, Hatfield wondered, and, even more important, what did it presage? Questions for which he greatly desired the answers. But how the devil to get them! All he could do was wait, and watch. He went back to patrolling the wire with little interest in the chore.

In fact, Hatfield felt that the patrol was very

much in the nature of a futile gesture. The area was too great for two, or even a half dozen riders to hope to cover effectively. And the wideloopers would have little difficulty spotting them and keeping them under surveillance while they went about their business.

However, he kept it up till the east was graying and then rode home to bed, neither knowing or giving a darn if Dudley had preceded him. He morosely admitted that the situation was getting more mixed up all the time, with so far no solution in sight.

Several quiet days followed. The patrols were constantly on the job, day and night, and nothing happened. Between routine range chores, Hatfield managed to examine the east wall of the valley. As he expected, he found that the cliffs extended in an unbroken line to its mouth. Nowhere was there a cleft or a slope by which cattle could be driven to the crest. And nowhere were the perpendicular walls of stone less than twenty-five or thirty feet high, in some places even more.

There was constant intercourse between the valley ranchers and Hatfield had the opportunity to meet the various owners and most of the hands. He quickly catalogued them as an average lot, honest, industrious, and unimaginative. Certainly none of them showed any evidence of being the mysterious master-mind who was keeping the section in a state of constant turmoil.

The Ranger learned one disquieting thing. Almost to a man the cattlemen were convinced that John Hardin and the farmers were to blame for their troubles. They stubbornly brushed aside all argument. Their minds were fixed. It was clear that their tempers were close to the breaking point. It would take very little to set off the explosion.

One evening Dudley remarked to Hatfield, 'Well, Jim, I reckon it's up to you and me to handle the patrol chore again. We'll do it same as last time. You take the east and I'll take the west.'

Hatfield rode east, all right, but he didn't ride far. Once he was sure there was little chance of his being observed, he circled back west and did not draw rein till he was sheltered by a clump of growth only a short distance from the cut wire. He made himself as comfortable as circumstances permitted and settled down to wait. There was no moon, but the sky was brilliant with stars that cast enough light over the rangeland to make objects clearly visible for a considerable distance.

Slowly and tediously the hours passed, and it was just about midnight when Hatfield's keen ears caught the sound of a horse approaching. A few minutes later Tom Dudley rode into view, pacing his horse slowly along the wire. He drew rein beside the cut panel, dismounted and unhooked the strands. Then he forked his horse and waited, lounging easily in the saddle. Hatfield watched the north, tense and expectant.

Very soon the rider from the north appeared, cutting along at a fast pace, veered through the open wire and drew rein beside Dudley. The starlight glinted on glossy curls as the two figures merged. Hatfield could, almost hear the long and passionate kiss!

CHAPTER FOURTEEN

Jim Hatfield removed his hat, rumpled his black hair and replaced the hat on his head with the utmost nicety. He cuffed it over his left eye and spoke a whisper into Goldy's ear.

'Now if this isn't the making of a story to tell on a train trip with a batch of travelling men! The rancher sparkin' the farmer's daughter! Nice, and romantic, and plumb interesting! But where does it leave me? All my nicely built up theories knocked into a cocked hat! I'm right back where I started. With Tom Dudley out of the picture and, in all probability, John Hardin out, too, all I've got left is one lead so loco it didn't appear worth considering. But now, through a process of eliminating all other suspects, maybe it isn't so loco after all. There they go! Riding off to mush it up someplace.'

Suddenly he chuckled, although he was in

little mood for mirth. Now he recalled how quick Verna Hardin had been to champion Tom Dudley as she and old John rode with him to the wire. Oh, he could see it all now—marvel of perspicacity! He settled down again to wait till the starry-eyed pair returned, which they did after considerable time had passed. After a last lingering embrace, Verna rode north. Dudley hooked up the wire and rode west. Hatfield rode east by south in a very bad temper.

But before he got back to the ranchhouse and bed he began to see some humor in the situation. The way old John would rare up on his hind legs and paws and when he learned what was going on would be a caution to cats. Well, it was evident that Verna had the old shorthorn pretty well under her small thumb, and although he would paw the hackamore a bit, doubtless she would be able to handle him.

And, the way things were shaping up, Hatfield felt that maybe there wouldn't be any range war, after all, if he could just manage to hold it off a bit.

But the mystery of the persistent cattle stealing that plagued the section was still a mystery, and Hatfield had but one slender and unsubstantiated lead to work on.

A couple more peaceful days passed. The Lazy D hands were becoming optimistic and cheerful.

'Maybe we've scared 'em off, with

everybody on their toes and keeping a close watch,' hazarded rotund, jolly Chuck Arbuckle.

'Don't you believe it,' replied the pessimistic Vibart. 'They'll be busting loose somewhere soon. Wouldn't be surprised if it happened tonight; I feel a hunch coming on.'

Jim Hatfield also suddenly had a hunch. He hadn't forgotten the band of horsemen who very nearly blew his head off the night he first rode down the valley, proof positive that somebody who didn't belong there did ride the valley during the dark hours. He decided to follow it.

'Tom,' he said, 'you'll remember we tracked two herds to just about the same spot on the trail. Maybe there was a reason for them being driven to that particular spot, a meeting place or something. What do you say, how about riding over there and hanging around for a few hours. Then if Vibart's hunch happens to be a straight one, we might hit on something. It isn't very late, just ten o'clock, and all we have to lose is a few hours sleep, and perhaps considerable to gain.'

'That's a notion,' Dudley instantly agreed. 'These work dodgers don't need sleep, that's all they do in their hulls all day. Let's go!'

Twenty minutes later, the Lazy D outfit, eleven strong, was riding south by west, under a sky brilliant with stars.

'Feels like rain,' Vibart observed. 'Air's

sultry as blazes and I thought I heard thunder, way oft, a minute ago.'

'Rain won't hurt you,' said Arbuckle, 'besides, you need a bath. Been quite a while since you fell in that waterhole over on the east pasture.'

They had covered only about three miles when Vibart suddenly uttered an exclamation. 'Look!' he said, 'ain't that cows coming from back of that grove?'

It was, about forty or fifty head, streaming from behind the clump of trees. Another moment and half a dozen horsemen bulged out of the shadows, shoving the cattle along.

'By God, it's them!' yelled Dudley. 'After the sidewinders!'

The cowboys whooped. The excited horses leaped forward; but it was instantly clear that they had been sighted. The wideloopers bunched together, then whirled their mounts and streaked away south by west. After them tore the Lazy D hands, yelling and cursing.

'They're heading for the trail,' jolted Vibart. 'They know they got to get out of the valley, and that's the only way.'

'We'll get 'em!' declared Dudley. 'We've got good horses. Just wait 'til we get in shooting distance.'

But it quickly became apparent that they weren't to get within shooting distance anyways soon. The outlaws were also well mounted and they were racing their horses.

When they reached the trail, a little later, they turned into it and thundered south.

The trail was not always straight and it was nervous business careening around the bulges ahead not knowing what might be waiting for them on the other side.

'Not likely to stop and shoot it out, though,' Hatfield said. 'They're outnumbered nearly two to one. And they can't turn off onto the range without us spotting them. Ride and keep on riding!'

A little later Dudley let out a shout. 'There's the Lucky Seven ranchhouse right ahead!' he exclaimed. 'Maybe we can rouse the boys up and they'll stop 'em.'

He jerked his gun as he spoke and began shooting at the fugitives. The other hands joined in, punctuating the reports with shrill whoops. A few answering flashes replied from the fleeing owl-hoots, but the distance was great and the only result was a most hellish racket.

Lights flashed up in the dark mass of the ranchhouse. There came faintly a sound of shouting. Dudley continued to shoot and yell.

'Too late!' Hatfield told him. 'They're past.'

But the ranch owner paid him no heed. 'Wideloopers!' he bellowed at the top of his voice. 'Stop 'em!'

At the thoroughly aroused ranchhouse, somebody cut loose with a shotgun. The Lazy D hands ducked as buckshot whistled over their heads.

'You gosh darned loco jugheads!' howled Dudley.

The second barrel of the shotgun was his answer, and the buckshot came closer.

'Ride!' thundered Hatfield. 'They don't know what it's all about and are taking a whack at every head that shows. Ride and don't try it again, it doesn't work.'

They quickly left the bee-bumbling ranchhouse behind, but in the confusion the horses had broken stride and the fugitives had gained.

The miles flowed under the pounding hoofs. They passed another dark ranchhouse, and did nothing to arouse its sleeping inhabitants. The horses were blowing now, but Hatfield knew the outlaws' mounts could be in no better shape, and slowly but surely the pursuit was gaining. Thunder was muttering beyond the wall of the western hills, but the stars still shone brightly.

Finally they saw, hanging above the mesa on which the town perched, the lights of Terligua.

'Maybe if we start shooting again they'll come out and stop 'em,' Chuck Arbuckle panted hopefully.

'Not a chance,' answered Vibart. 'They're too used to fool punchers skalleyhooting into town and shooting holes in the sky. They wouldn't even look up from their drinks.'

'Wonder if they'll turn west on the trail or

keep on heading south?' said Dudley. Nobody had the answer.

The fugitives provided it as they flashed past the mesa. They crossed the east-west trail and continued straight down the depression Hatfield knew was a continuation of the ancient river bed.

'We'll get 'em!' exulted Dudley. 'This dry wash runs for miles, and they won't dare run off to climb the slopes. That would slow 'em up.'

Hatfield nodded and anxiously glanced westward. The rumble of distant thunder was loudening and now that they were beyond the obstructing cliffs he could see a heavy cloud bank climbing slowly up the slant of the sky. There was a storm coming, all right, although it still seemed a long ways off.

But the light was dimming as the steadily climbing cloud bank obscured more and more of the stars. The forms ahead were becoming shadowy.

The panting horses had slowed to a canter. Goldy alone still appeared comparatively fresh. Hatfield debated whether to give him his head and close the distance to accurate shooting range, but reluctantly decided against the move as too foolhardy, odds of six to one were a bit on the heavy side. He'd very likely just succeed in getting himself killed and accomplish nothing. Besides, they were undoubtedly shortening the distance between them and the laboring horses of the outlaws.

And then without warning the storm burst. There came a howling blast of wind, and on its wings a veritable cloudburst of rain. Instantly the landscape was blotted out as if a curtain had been drawn. Nothing was visible a foot beyond a horse's nose.

Drenched, blinded and deafened, the cowboys bent their beads to the fury of the blast, their cursing voices thin and reedy as the piping of insects in the turmoil of wind and rain and crashing thunder. The lightning flashes only served to dazzle their eyes and further confuse their senses.

'Keep on slugging ahead!' Hatfield shouted above the uproar. 'They're catching it just as bad as we are and they're not likely to turn off.'

For perhaps ten minutes the storm continued with unabated fury; then it ceased almost as suddenly as it began. The wind dropped, the rain stopped falling, the western sky brightened. The stars came out and their light revealed no sign of the fugitives. But the tracks left by their horses showed plainly in the wet sand.

'Might as well follow them for a bit and maybe learn where they're heading,' Hatfield decided.

For a short distance the tracks continued south, then they turned sharply and climbed the gentle western slope. Upon reaching its crest, they veered more and more to the north

'Heading for the east-west trail, sure as blazes,' said Dudley. Hatfield nodded and did not comment.

They reached the trail, cut by a myriad of hoofs and rutted by wagon wheels. Hatfield scanned it and shook his head. He dismounted, drew matches from a tightly corked bottle and managed to strike one inside the dry lock of his Winchester. By the flickering flame he examined the ground at close range.

'I think they headed west, but I'm not sure,' he said. 'Doesn't make much difference which direction they went, anyhow.'

'Shall we follow them?' asked Dudley.

'Would be just a waste of time,' Hatfield told him. 'When they dropped out of sight we lost them. We haven't the slightest notion who we were chasing. If they came riding back this way right now we couldn't do a thing. Because we wouldn't know for sure it was them, much less be able to prove it.'

'Guess you're right,' Dudley agreed gloomily. 'Well reckon we might as well head for town and a drink. I could sure stand a snort about now.'

'Just where do you figure we are right now?' Hatfield asked as he forked Goldy.

Dudley glanced about. 'I'd say we're about a couple of miles east of Ellis Gault's ranchhouse,' he replied. 'Think it would be a good idea to ride over there and ask him if he heard them go past?'

'What good would it do if he did hear them?' Hatfield objected. 'I don't suppose he's in the habit of running out every time somebody rides past his place to ask them who they are and where they're going.'

'Reckon you're right again,' Dudley admitted. 'Oh, tarnation! Let's head for town.'

The Lazy D hands were mightily disgruntled over their failure to come up with the wideloopers, but Jim Hatfield felt it had been a pretty good night's work. His vague, inchoate lead was abruptly beginning to assume something of form and substance.

But if Ellis Gault was his man, he was still a hell of a long ways from being in a position to drop a loop on him. He conned over carefully the various incidents that served to point the finger of suspicion at Gault. First, by a process of elimination, his suspects dropping out of the picture one by one, Gault was the only individual he had contacted who showed indications of having the brains and ability necessary to direct the depredations taking place in the section. Which, of course, didn't mean much. The real culprit might well be keeping under cover to an extent that he, Hatfield, had not yet contacted him at all. Of this, however, Hatfield was doubtful. The nature of the criminal operations suggested strongly that whoever was directing them was somebody thoroughly familiar with conditions in and around Escondida Valley and in a position to easily acquire pertinent information. Which would not be the case with an out-of-the-section brush popper holed up somewhere.

Next, prior to each of the three attempts on his life, Gault had been in his presence. Just coincidence, perhaps, but something to consider. Most significant was the drygulching on the east-west trail. A rider neither Hatfield nor Dudley saw had slipped away from the Boxed E ranchhouse shortly after their arrival, ostensibly to notify Preston that the Lazy D hands would come for the cows he had for sale, but Hatfield had gathered from the subsequent conversation with Gault that the stock was ready and waiting for delivery, so why was it necessary to notify Preston, and in such a hurry? More guesswork, of course, but all he had to rely on, so far, was guesswork.

And tonight. It was obvious to Hatfield that the wideloopers had a hide-out somewhere west of Terligua, a place that must be kept a secret at all costs. Because of which they had taken the chance on riding south through the open depression where there was no cover, when they could just as easily have turned west on the trail once they cleared the valley. Along that trail were plenty of places where they would have had an excellent opportunity to slip into the chaparral with a chance of losing their pursuers, opportunities that certainly did not afford along the route they chose. It appeared logical that they banked on the coming storm to cover their movements long enough to allow them to ride up the slope of the wash, turn north and reach the trail that ran past Gault's ranchhouse. Which was just what happened. Of course he had no proof that they stopped at the Boxed E ranchhouse, but it was another tie-up.

All of which was pleasant and comfortable theorizing, but he still had no explanation of how the stolen cattle were slipped out of the guarded valley, and nothing definite to show that Gault had anything to do with it. Well, it was up to him to find out. That was what he was here for. He dismissed the problem for the moment as the lights of Terligua showed in the distance.

The Lazy D hands quickly had the Montezuma in an uproar with their graphic accounts of the night's misadventure. This was not lessened by the arrival soon afterward of Sam Lawson soaked to the skin and in a very bad temper.

'I caught on to what was in the wind,' he told Hatfield, 'but not soon enough to keep our cook, who's even crazier than Hassayampa Jones, from throwing down on you with his scattergun. Hope he didn't nick anybody.'

'We heard 'em whistle, but that was all,' Dudley put in. 'We muffed a fine chance to corral some of the sidewinders tonight, Sam, but anyway I reckon we threw a scare into them. Maybe they'll lay off for a while.'

'Which way did you say those cows were headed when you first spotted them?' Lawson asked.

'Toward the trail,' Dudley replied.

'And I'll bet they were veering to the north,' Lawson added pointedly. Dudley was forced to admit it was so.

An ominous silence followed Lawson's remark, then fierce wrangles and discussion broke out all over the saloon.

CHAPTER FIFTEEN

Daylight was streaking the sky when the weary Lazy D riders got back to the ranchhouse.

'Tumble into bed and get a few hours sleep,' Dudley told them. 'Then we've got to get busy on that shipping herd. I got the order and they want 'em on time. The Lucky Seven is also getting a herd ready and we'll make the drive together. Safer that way, they'll be more of us along.'

For the shipping herd, Tom Dudley chose his beefs carefully. Only the very best stuff was assembled in close herd on the Lazy D southwest pasture. Even average and better-than-middlin' stock was cut out and allowed to

148

drift back on the range.

'The Armon people want only high-grade beef cows,' Dudley explained to Hatfield. 'They pack fancy stuff and are mighty finicky as to what they get, but they pay top prices and no haggling. They're sort of partial to this section with its improved stock. Wouldn't touch a mossyback longhorn with a ten-foot pole.'

Finally the shipping herd was complete to the owner's satisfaction. Dudley looked over the assembled cows with pardonable pride.

'Never saw a better looking bunch,' he declared, 'and the Lucky Seven has better than a hundred critters almost as good. Quite a drive, three hundred and more head.'

'Would be nice pickings for an owlhoot bunch,' remarked Vibart.

'Uh-huh, and just let 'em try it,' said Dudley. 'I've a notion we sort of scared 'em off last week. Not a head been lost from the valley since then.'

'Just wait,' grunted Vibart.

'You're always bellyaching, Walt,' said Dudley. 'You haven't even been satisfied with the plumb fine weather we've had for this chore.'

'It won't last,' replied the pessimist. 'Liable to rain all the way from here to Persimmon Gap. Betcha it rains tonight.'

'Be good for the grass,' Dudley answered cheerfully. 'Well, let's head back for the *casa*

149

and something to eat. Hassayampa's got the chuck wagon ready and loaded, snakes and all.'

After they had finished eating supper, Hatfield made a suggestion. 'Tom,' he said, 'we want to get an early start tomorrow anyhow, so why not camp tonight in that grove beside the holding spot? That way we'd be all set to go by daylight and not hold up the Lucky Seven boys. They said they'd wait for us before heading for the trail. And we'd be in a position to keep a close watch on that valuable herd, just in case.'

'It's a notion,' Dudley agreed. 'I'd figured on three or four night guards to keep watch, but that'll be even better. That way one night hawk on a four hour trick will be enough and everybody can get a good rest. We'll do it.'

Nobody objected and the Lazy D bunch made a comfortable night camp in the grove. No fires were lighted for it was warm.

'Better not to advertise our presence, just in case,' Hatfield explained.

The night passed peacefully enough except that Walt Vibart proved himself a reliable weather prophet. Shortly after midnight the weather underwent a sudden and unexpected change. Hatfield awoke to a crash of thunder and a roar of rain hammering the leaves over his head. The others awoke also, and there was considerable profanity, mostly directed at the head of the luckless Vibart, his companions declaring his danged croaking had brought on the storm. But the hardy cowboys were accustomed to sleeping out in all kinds of weather. Snugged in their waterproof ponchos they didn't do so badly. For about twenty minutes the storm raged, with water descending in sheets. Then the squall ended suddenly, leaving a clean washed sky glittering with stars. Everybody went back to sleep.

*　　　*　　　*

At the Lucky Seven holding spot, only a few miles distant to the south, things were grimly different. Sam Lawson had assigned three thoroughly reliable hands, Mulligan, Raines, and McGregor, to the chore of night guarding the comparatively small herd, while he and the rest of his hands slept at the ranchhouse.

'And don't go to sleep and let those cows stray,' Lawson warned the night hawks. 'If we have to round 'em up again in the morning I'll skin the three of you till you look like the American Flag. We'll be with you before the sun's up.'

The three hands found little to do. Occasionally an ambitious cow would develop a yearning for far-off places and attempt to stray, only to be shunted ignominiously back to the pasture.

For the most part the critters were content to graze or stand pensively in the pool formed by the widening of a little stream. As darkness descended they bunched and finally lay down with contented rumblings.

The cowboys lounged about, smoking, and talking. They anticipated no trouble with the cattle, or any other kind, for that matter. Despite the epidemic of rustling in the valley, no guarded herd had ever been molested. Easier and safer to pick up stray bunches was the prevailing opinion. The hands cooked their simple meal over a small fire and smoked some more. Towards ten o'clock they mounted their horses and rode slowly around the herd to make sure everything was okay, pausing for a gab when they met in the course of their rounds.

The night was still, the sky glittering with myriad stars. In the west was a slight film of haze that climbed slowly up along the slant of the heavens. Over the western hills was an occasional fitful glow that reddened the haze for an instant. No leaf stirred in the thickets, the grasses stood stiffly erect. The growth that hemmed the pasture was black and formless in the faint light of the stars.

The three cowboys met not far from the dark wall of chapparal to the west. Lounging comfortably in their saddles, they rolled cigarettes and smoked in silence. McGregor suddenly lifted his head and glanced toward the shadowy thickets.

'Thought I heard something over there,' he

commented.

'Some little critter, or maybe a bird fell off his perch,' guessed Raines.

'There it is again,' exclaimed McGregor, a moment later. 'Say, that sounds like a horse's . . .'

He never completed the sentence. His companions would not have heard him if he had.

For from the silent growth burst a roar of gunfire. Red flashes gushed from the thicket, again and again.

The three night hawks went down without a cry. Silent and motionless they lay in the tall grass, unseeing eyes glaring upward stonily at the star strewn sky.

From the thicket rode a dozen shadowy shapes. Quickly they quieted the alarmed cows and started them moving westward in close herd. The muffled click of irons and the pad of unshod hoofs died away. Silence shrouded the pasture. An inquisitive rodent crept from under a bush and stared with beady eyes at the three awful forms lying so motionless in the tall grass. A horse pawed the ground. Another whinnied mournfully. Then the silence descended again like a shroud.

*   *   *

The Lucky Seven hands, Sam Lawson at their head, left the ranchhouse before daybreak.

Soon they were riding gaily through a world brilliant with sunshine and fragrant with the smells of the rain cleansed grass. They swept around a grove and approached the holding spot.

'Where in blazes are those cows?' a puncher suddenly yelped.

'And where are the night hawks?' demanded another.

They found the three night hawks without difficulty, what was left of them, which was enough for a burial and nothing more. They had been shot to pieces. Their bodies lay sprawled stiffly on the damp grass. Their horses, still saddled and bridled, grazed a little way off. The herd was nowhere in sight.

Cursing viciously, the cowboys dismounted and grouped around their slain fellows.

'Hold it!' ordered Lawson, his face set like granite. 'Don't touch anything. And keep your broncs bunched so they won't track up the ground. Ferguson, you ride to the Lazy D holding spot, they should be under way by now, and don't spare your horse. Get them down here as fast as you can. Maybe Hatfield can make something of this and follow the trail those infernal rattlesnakes left, if there is one. They say he's a whizzer at it. Get going!'

The Lazy D herd was under way, when Ferguson rode up on his lathered horse and gulped out his story. Leaving one hand to see that the cows did not stray unduly, the outfit rode south at a fast pace.

'Don't push the horses too hard,' Hatfield warned. 'We might need them,' he added significantly.

When they reached the Lucky Seven pasture, Hatfield dismounted and examined the bodies.

'They were killed before the rain started,' he announced.

'How do you know?' asked Dudley.

'Grass beneath the bodies is almost dry, and broken by their falling on it,' the Lone Wolf explained. 'Looks like they never had a chance. Mowed down from the edge of thicket over there when they stopped to gab a minute in the course of their ride around the herd.'

'Think you can track the darned sidewinders?' asked Lawson.

'No chance across the prairie,' Hatfield replied. 'The rain beat the grass down and destroyed all prints; but I've a hunch they headed for the trail. If they did, that rain gave us a break. Hoofs would have scored deep in the mud and there wouldn't be any cows over there this early to mess them up. I've a notion the hellions didn't figure on that unexpected rain, not a sign of it yesterday evening or they wouldn't have done the chore last night. It may prove their undoing. Let's go. We'll ride straight for the trail and see what we can find.'

'And when we find the tracks, they'll lead north,' Lawson declared bitterly.

'Don't bull ahead and jump at conclusions,' Hatfield told him sternly.

Lawson subsided to wordless rumblings. His companions rode in stony silence.

In less than an hour they reached the trail. Hatfield nodded with satisfaction.

'There they are,' he said. 'Prints of cows and horses, too, cut so deep anybody could follow them.'

'And they're pointing north!' Lawson exclaimed. What did I tell you?'

'And don't forget what I told you,' Hatfield answered in a voice that silenced the range boss.

Faces grim, the massed cowboys swept north along the trail. The fresh tracks flowed steadily before them, deeply scored in the mud left by the hard rain. They soon reached a patch of stony ground, however, and here the prints were not so plain, but there were enough markings on softer spots to assure Hatfield that the herd had not turned off onto the prairie.

The trail curved steadily around a wide shoulder of the encroaching cliff. As they surged ahead, Hatfield suddenly held up his hand.

'Horses!' exclaimed Dudley. 'Coming from the north and coming fast!'

'Careful,' Hatfield cautioned, 'don't go off half-cocked, but be ready for business. Slow down a little.'

At a somewhat reduced speed, the bunched riders surged around the curve of the trail. And around the bend from the north bulged a full score of dark-faced horsemen. At their head rode John Hardin!

Shouting and cursing, the two troops jerked their horses to a sliding halt within twenty feet of each other.

'There they are!' bawled John Hardin. 'The infernal cow thieves!'

'Cow thieves!' Sam Lawson howled in reply. 'Why you mangy old widelooper! What'd you do with our beefs?'

There was a clutching of weapons on both sides, but Jim Hatfield's voice rolled in thunder above the turmoil, 'Stop it! Dudley, Jackson, hold your men! Hardin, take your hand off your gun!'

He sent Goldy charging forward as he spoke, and came to a pause between the two factions.

'What's the matter with you, Hardin?' he demanded. 'What do you mean by skalleyhooting down here on the prod?'

'I tell you the danged horned toads stole my cows!' Hardin bellowed. 'They cut my wire and run off half my herd. We've been tracking them down this way all morning.'

'And we've been tracking ours up this way!' shouted Sam Lawson.

'Shut up, all of you!' Hatfield thundered again. 'I'm going to do the talking and I'll

157

pistol whip the first man who opens his mouth to argue before I've finished.'

'Hold it, boys,' cautioned Lawson. 'He means it.'

'Yes, and he can do it,' rumbled John Hardin. 'I got good reason to know.'

Surprisingly, it was impulsive, hot-tempered Sam Lawson who made the first move to support Hatfield.

'I don't know what's going on or what it's all about,' he said, 'but 'I 'low Hatfield has more savvy than all the rest of us put together. Me, I'm backing his play. Go ahead, Jim, we're listening.'

'Hardin, you say you tracked your cows down this way,' Hatfield said after quiet had ensued. 'Well, look at the ground in front of you. Do you see any tracks heading south? I don't. But there are still tracks headed north. Get down and look for yourself.'

Old John, rumbling and grunting, slid from his saddle and scanned the ground at his feet.

'Tarnation, you're right!' he admitted. 'But the tracks show plain up above, on the soft ground. The trail from here north to my place ain't hardly ever used any more, except by loafing cows, and those fresh iron prints stand our like a cowhand in church.'

'And you didn't notice they stopped after you hit the hard ground,' Hatfield remarked quietly, 'Did you notice any tracks going north the other side of this stretch? You could hardly have missed them in the mud.'

'There wasn't any,' Hardin declared with conviction.

'All right,' Hatfield said. 'Then it looks like they must have turned off somewhere between here and the softer ground farther up. We're heading up that way slow, all of us. Come along, and no nonsense. Wait till I get in front.'

He sent his horse through the ranks of Hardin's glowering *vaqueros*, who instinctively opened up to let him pass. With both outfits following closely behind, he led the way north, searching every foot of the ground with his eyes. Less than three hundred yards farther on, where the trail abruptly straightened out, he pulled up, the others jostling to a halt behind him, and pointed to the ground.

The soil was hard and rocky, but a multitude of confused prints showed, especially on the softer outer edge of the trail.

'Here's where the two herds came together,' he said. 'Anybody with half an eye can see that. If you hadn't been hightailing like you were, Hardin, you would have noticed it.'

Old John swore a complicated oath. 'Danged if you ain't right again,' he admitted.

'Then they must have turned east,' Lawson exclaimed excitedly. 'Turned east and curved around to the south, after the two herds came together. But how in blazes would they get past the boys patrolling the range down there?'

'Maybe those fellers holed up during the

rain and didn't come out again,' hazarded a Lucky Seven hand.

'Could be, but very unlikely,' said Tom Dudley. 'Hatfield, do you think you can track the herd across the range?'

Hatfield gazed at the tall and thick grass and shook his head dubiously. 'I doubt it,' he said. 'The grass must have been a regular mat after it was beaten down by the rain and when the sun dried it out, it sprang up again and hid everything. But we'll make a try at it. Everybody unfork and get busy.'

Hatfield knew very well there was not a chance to pick up a trail across the rangeland, if there was one, but something to do would give tempers a chance to cool, especially with the two outfits handling the chore together. His own examination of the soil was perfunctory. The stubborn overgrown grass covered the soil in a dense mat that defied the beat of a passing hoof to leave a trace. But as he glanced around a pleased expression brightened his green eyes. Mutual misfortune appeared to be drawing the two outfits together. He saw a cowhand pass the makin's to a *vaquero* and accept a light in return. Even John Hardin and Sam Lawson were grunting something at each other with wagging heads.

'Looks like some good may come out of this mess, after all,' he muttered, 'but where in the name of blue blazes did those cows go?'

He raised his eyes to the far wall of the

valley, knowing very well what he would find there.

Glittering in the morning sunlight, it fanged upward from the more regular contours of the eastern hills, a naked spire of stone. For the third time he had tracked a stolen herd to this identical point of the trail. What in the devil did it mean!

He turned and stared at the gray ribs of rock that formed the cliffs, as if expecting them to melt away before his eyes and show an easy route to their crests.

They didn't. They stood gray and immutable, guarding their secret well. He examined their surface with a searching gaze. Everywhere they were uniformly the same, solid, unbroken, these ancient ramparts that had once walled in a river. Here they were a bit lower than at some other points, not much more than twenty feet in height, but perfectly sheer.

His eyes reached the crest and travelled along it. It was slightly ragged, with the fronds of growth waving over it, and everywhere the same, except—directly opposite where he stood a whitish patch, a foot or so in width, stood out against the uniform gray. Evidently a bit of the lip had either sloughed off or had been broken off recently. He dropped his eyes to the trail. At the foot of the cliff lay a bit of talus, one side showing a clean white line of cleavage. Undoubtedly it had fallen from above, broken off in some way from the parent rock. A funny thing to happen for no reason that he could see. The clean break showed it had not weathered off. Looked more like a sudden hard blow had loosened it.

Hatfield hadn't the remotest idea what it might mean, but abruptly he decided to find out at the first opportunity. Anyplace else and he wouldn't have given it a second thought, but right here where three times he had tracked a vanished herd, made it of much importance.

The disgusted cowboys were straggling back to the trail. 'No soap,' growled Lawson, 'we're just wasting our time.'

'My sentiments,' rumbled Hardin. 'We might as well go home. Fork your broncs, *muchachos*, and let's get going.'

Hatfield paused beside Hardin. 'I'll be riding up to see you soon, sir,' he said.

'Do that,' Hardin urged. 'I sure want to talk to you. Verna'll be mighty glad to see you, too.'

With a wave of his hand he rode north, his men following. Hatfield noticed with satisfaction that several of these waved to the cowboys, who returned the salutation.

Tom Dudley rode up. 'Well, I reckon we'd better head back and get that trail herd moving,' he said wearily. 'Maybe we can shove it to Terligua before dark and corral it there for the night. We're going to be late for delivery if we don't hustle, and the cattle cars will be piling up demurrage.'

'I'm plumb sorry about what happened, Sam,' he told Lawson, 'but I reckon there's nothing we can do.'

'Reckon not,' agreed the Lucky Seven range boss. 'But what I want to know is where in blazes did those cows get to? John Hardin didn't have 'em in his back pocket, that's sure for certain. A darn shame he had to lose that stock of his. I've heard about those critters he breeds, no finer cows in Texas.'

Hatfield suppressed a smile. Yes, some good was coming from the night of tragedy, a night that could have easily developed into an even greater tragedy. For the significance of the puzzling wire cutters he had taken from the dead dryglucher's pocket, on the trail from Ellis Gault's ranch, was very plain now.

As they rode back to the herd, Hatfield reflected on what he alone had realized and understood: the simple but utterly devilish scheme devised and carried out by the outlaw bunch. Cut John Hardin's wire and run south as many of his cows as they could handle. At the same time, lift the Lucky Seven herd and run it north. Hardin would come raging south in pursuit of his stolen stock. The cowboys would ride north. The two groups would meet, a bloody corpse-and-cartridge session would ensue, and the whole valley would be aflame.

And only the presence of mind and outstanding personality of the Lone Wolf had prevented the tragedy!

CHAPTER SIXTEEN

The Lucky Seven hands departed to bury their dead. Dudley and his men picked up the shipping herd and headed south, reaching the mouth of the valley a little after dark. They laid over in Terligua till the following morning.

The drive to Marton by way of the Comanche Trail and Persimmon Gap was uneventful. But it was a long, hard pull and took three days. Dudley fretted over the weight his slow and heavy cows were losing, but there was nothing to be done about it. Finally they reached Marton at nightfall of the third day and corralled the herd. The next morning the beefs were driven to the loading pens and safely stowed in the cattle cars waiting on the siding.

The Lazy D outfit repaired to Mexican Pete's place for a few drinks and something to eat before starting the long trip home. They had nearly finished their meal when a big man with a scowling face shoved through the swinging doors and strode over to their table. It was John Hardin.

'Howdy, Hatfield,' he said, pointedly ignoring the others. 'See you got your beefs all loaded. Ready to go home? You might as well head south across my holdings. No sense in taking that long ride by way of the Gap.'

'How about the wire?' Hatfield asked, his face sober but his eyes dancing.

'There ain't no wire across that danged trail any more,' Hardin snorted. 'The devil with it! And keep your blamed horses out of my alfalfa!'

He spun on his heel and stalked out, leaving the punchers staring after him in slack-jawed amazement.

'Well, I'll—I'll—I'll be danged!' sputtered Tom Dudley.

'Wouldn't be surprised,' Hatfield agreed cheerfully. 'Well, if you jiggers have finished eating, let's have that last drink and head for home. We should make it before dark, by way of the valley.'

'Tarnation, maybe it's a trap!' exclaimed the suspicious Vibart. 'Maybe he figures to line us up against the wire and mow us down.'

I guess we can risk it,' Hatfield replied. 'Ready to go?'

The cowboys were a bit nervous as they rode over Hardin's land, but they did not meet a single *vaquero* on the way, nor anybody else for that matter. When they reached the wire that formerly spanned the trail, they found it cut at the posts.

'Danged if the old jigger didn't mean it,' marvelled Vibart. 'What's come over him, anyhow? Has he got religion?'

'Something like that, I'd say,' Hatfield smiled.

They reached the Lazy D shortly after dark. Hassayampa, the cook, who with difficulty had been kept sober, gave profane instructions as to the care of his beloved chuck wagon and hobbled in to get supper.

Later in the evening, Hatfield approached Dudley. 'Tom,' he said, 'I'd like to take a little ride to town tomorrow. Might want to stay overnight. Is it okay?'

'Sure it's okay,' Dudley instantly responded. If anybody around here deserves a few days lay-off, it's you. You do more work in one day than any of the rest of those leadpants terrapins do in three. Go ahead and have yourself a good bust, and don't hurry back.'

Hatfield slept late the following morning. After enjoying a leisurely breakfast he got the rig on Goldy and rode south.

He took his time and it was growing dark when he reached Terligua. He stabled his horse and loafed around the town for several hours, visiting the Montezuma and other places and generally playing the part of a cowhand with a day off.

One of the Lazy D hands had ridden to town early in the morning to do a chore, and the whole pueblo was buzzing over the news that John Hardin had opened the trail through the valley. Hatfield listened to the various comments with satisfaction. No matter what

166

else happened, one thing was now certain; there wasn't going to be a range war in Escondida Valley.

*   *   *

Midnight found him in the saddle again. His pouches contained a small skillet, a little flat bucket, a slab of bacon, some eggs carefully wrapped against breakage, and several of Hassayampa's biscuits. He was all set for a day and a night out.

He rode north till he reached the trail that ran past the valley mouth, then he turned west, riding swiftly for several miles. Where the chaparral cast a deep shadow he pulled to one side and sat motionless for some time, to make sure he had not been followed. Satisfied that he was not wearing a tail, he sought out one of the dim trails that wound upward through the growth and followed it till he found a spot where a little spring bubbled from under a rock and sparse grass grew. Here he got the rig off Goldy and turned him loose to graze. With his saddle for a pillow, he stretched out on a bed of dead leaves and was soon fast asleep.

He arose in the gray of the morning, before sunrise, when the smoke of his small fire of dry wood was less likely to be seen. He had no desire to advertise his presence. From such an outfit as he was up against, possibly prowling the bills in the dark hours, he knew he could

167

expect no mercy. Staying alive meant staying under cover so far as was possible.

Soon bacon and eggs were sizzling in the skillet, a bucket of coffee steaming and bubbling. He ate his simple breakfast with the appetite of youth and perfect physical condition, smoked a cigarette and got the rig on Goldy.

'Well, horse, here we go,' he told the sorrel. 'We're going to, make a prime try at finding out what the devil's going on in this section, and I've a notion we're going to find out. I'm getting a hunch as to just how those cows are whisked, a notion that's just exactly how— through the air! Let's go!'

The snaky trail, which Hatfield quickly decided was nothing more than a game track, turned and twisted and doubled back on itself but maintained a steady upward trend. The sun was well up in the sky when he finally neared the crest of the long ridge that was the backbone of the range of hills. And here the game track flowed into another and very ancient trail, this time a definite trail, narrow but scored deep in the soil. Doubtless it had been beaten long years ago by the pad of countless moccasined feet. A trail followed by Indians with designs on whoever or whatever lived in the lush valley below.

And now, while the smooth and level floor of the depression, softly carpeted with dead leaves, provided comfortable going for Goldy,

Hatfield was anything but comfortable. On the ridge crest the growth was much thinner, often there was none at all, and he knew that at times he was clearly outlined against the brilliant blue of the sky, a perfect target for anybody lurking on the slopes to the west.

'Horse, I've got a cold feeling up and down my backbone,' he complained to the placid sorrel. 'Every time you snap a stick, I nearly jump out of the hull. You're lucky, you old grass burner, not to be cursed with an imagination.'

Goldy didn't argue the point, but he shook his head as a token of general disagreement and plodded on.

Across the valley and to the north, Hatfield could see the glittering spire of rock standing out clear and hard against the sky. As he rode, the angle slowly broadened and after a while had become very nearly straight, evidence that he was drawing directly in line with his landmark. Almost straight down the eastern slope, now, should be the spot where the vanished herds reached the trail.

The old track wound through a thick bristle of brush, cleared the outer straggle, and Hatfield jerked Goldy to a halt.

Almost under the sorrel's nose was another trail, a fairly broad and well traveled trail scored and rutted by the hoofs of cattle and the irons of horses, some of them fairly fresh prints scored deep in the soil softened by the

169

heavy rain of less than a week before.

And the trail that dipped over the ridge and continued westward, also ran straight down the hill slope to the cliff tops below.

'Horse,' Hatfield said, 'this is it. This is the way those cows came, but we still don't know how the devil the sidewinders got 'em up top the cliffs. Let's go see.'

Riding with the utmost caution, every sense at hair-trigger alertness, he proceeded down the eastern slope. In a very short time he reined Goldy in on the crest of the low cliffs that flanked the trail down Escondida Valley.

Before dismounting he glanced about. Back from the cliff lip a little ways the brush was crushed and broken and trodden down. The spot where the cows were held in close herd. And straight to the cliff edge the trail ran to end in a wild jumble of prints and gouges, among which, Hatfield noted with a quickening eye, were the marks left by high-heeled boots.

With a final careful glance around, he dismounted and strode to the ragged lip of the cliff. Twenty feet below lay the trail, and directly in line across the valley was the glittering spire of naked stone.

His pulses quickening with anticipation, Hatfield began a thorough examination of his immediate surroundings.

Growing close to the lip of the cliff he found two sturdy trees standing less than eight feet apart and directly in line. Deep and wide notches had been cut near the base of each, circling the trunks. The inner surfaces of these notches were shredded and worn, as if some heavy object had ground hard against them.

Hatfield studied the peculiar notches, shook his head and continued his search; he was beginning to anticipate what he would find. Lying in a nearby thicket he discovered two roughly squared and heavy timbers about fifteen feet in length. They were firmly bolted together to form an open V. In the small open end of the V was a large iron pulley, grooved to accommodate a rope, its stout steel spindle secured accurately to the slanting timbers, so that the pulley turned freely and easily. It was nothing more nor less than a strong and heavy shears.

His eyes glowing, Hatfield continued to poke about. Carelessly concealed in the brush he found the rest of the contraption, a large and powerful windlass, the barrel turning between straddled saw-horse arrangements, so that the windlass could be easily moved and set up wherever desired. Around the barrel was wound a light but very strong cable of the best manila twist. To the end of the rope were spliced long and broad leather straps carefully padded with canvas and buckled to form big loops.

And there it was. The butt ends of the shears would be placed in the notches cut in the tree trunks and lashed loosely in place, the pulley extending over the lip of the cliff. The windlass would be set in place, the rope run across the pulley. Down on the trail, the strap loops would be buckled around a steer, fore and aft, and the animal easily raised by means of the windlass. Then the shears would be swung around and the critter dropped on the cliff top. By means of a similar contrivance Hatfield had seen several hundred head of cattle loaded into a ship's hold in record time. He estimated that a hundred head of stock could easily be lifted to the cliff top in little more than an hour. With that windlass two men could turn over a house.

With wild longhorns the task would be difficult if not impossible, but with the docile, improved stock of the valley, tame as pet cats, there was nothing to it. Trained horses could also be lifted just as easily. No wonder the wideloopers were able to get in and out of the valley without being detected.

A new wrinkle in cow stealing, all right, but perfectly adapted to the unusual physical features of Escondida Valley. Simple and ingenious, its very simplicity indicated that it was the scheme of a keen, resourceful and imaginative mind. The kind of a mind not often met with in cattleland.

With a last comprehensive glance around, that took in every detail of his surroundings, Hatfield mounted his horse and rode back up the trail. His next task was to learn where that trail led to, a rather ticklish chore. For him, if he happened to meet somebody on it, it might well lead to the next world.

He crossed the exposed crest and breathed a sigh of relief as the bristle of tall growth crowded close once more. Down the far slope the trail wound, through chaparral so thick that it would be invisible to anyone passing only a few yards distant.

Hatfield rode cautiously, slowing at every bend, pausing often to listen for any untoward sound ahead. After two hours of riding he reined in on the crest of a long sag that rumbled steeply downward. Far below he could see a square of green and gold gleaming in the sunlight—the growing crops on the mesa Ellis Gault had reclaimed from the desert. Over to one side were the buildings of the Boxed E ranch.

The trail continued down the slope almost to the mesa, but before reaching it, it curved sharply to the right and disappeared from his sight, leading, doubtless, to the hidden holding spot for the stolen herds.

It was ridiculous for him to ride further. He would be in plain view from the Boxed E ranchhouse and other buildings. And, in fact, nothing was to be gained from doing so. He gazed across the rangeland, toward the jumble of mountains and deserts criss-crossed by furtive trails that led to New Mexico and the

173

land below the Rio Grande, where there were always lucrative markets for stolen cattle. His glance dropped to the cluster of buildings on the mesa. His voice was almost regretful when he spoke to his horse.

'Strange, isn't it, feller, that a man can't be satisfied with the good he's got, but has to go reaching for more. Well, *amigo* Gault, it looks like you're nearing the end of the trail. Now if I can just set a proper trap for you, and if you'll be nice enough to walk into it, as I think you will, my chore in this section should be just about finished.'

Turning Goldy, he rode back up the trail, in search of a comfortable spot to hole up 'til dark. At this stage of the game it would not do to be seen riding out of the hills. When he left his place of concealment he took no chances but circled Terligua and rode into town from the east. After seeing that his horse was properly cared for and eating a meal in the Montezuma, he went to bed and slept 'til after sunrise the following morning. Late afternoon found him back at the Lazy D ranchhouse.

CHAPTER SEVENTEEN

That evening Tom Dudley appeared nervous and ill at ease. The patrols along Hardin's wire had been abandoned and the Lazy D watchers were concentrating on the south pastures. Hatfield watched him with amusement, knowing he was trying to figure out an excuse for getting away. Finally Dudley, apparently not being able to contrive a subtle approach, resorted to direct methods.

'I think I'll take a little ride,' he announced casually. 'It's a nice night and I can't seem to get sleepy.'

'Not a bad notion,' Hatfield agreed, adding mischievously 'want me to go along?'

'Oh, you needn't bother,' Dudley returned, even more casually. 'I imagine you're tired after your bust last night.'

'Okay,' Hatfield replied. 'Tell Verna hello for me.'

Dudley fairly leaped out of his chair. 'W-what the devil!' he stuttered.

'And I've been thinking,' Hatfield went on, sober-faced, 'that you two yearlings have waited about long enough. There's a preacher at Terligua, you know, and I figure tomorrow would be a good day for you to start pulling in double harness.'

Dudley sank back into his chair with a gasp. 'Say,' he demanded, 'is there anything you don't know?'

'Plenty,' Hatfield admitted, 'but I think I know what's right and proper in this case.'

Dudley's brow wrinkled in a worried frown. 'But what the devil will Hardin say? I'm afraid he'll go through the ceiling, and I don't want to

175

cause a bust-up between them. Verna's mighty fond of the old pelican, because he's her father, I suppose.'

'He can't get out of that,' Hatfield replied. 'Too great a similarity of disposition.'

'Guess he'd better not try it,' said Dudley. 'Hatfield, I'm danged if I won't do it. I don't believe Verna will object too strongly.'

'You tell her for me that I said she'd better not. I figure to ride up there in the next day or two,' Hatfield answered.

'Now what the devil do you mean by that?' Dudley asked perplexedly.

Hatfield grinned and didn't explain.

'Get going,' he said. 'You don't want to keep the lady waiting.

'And Tom,' he added, as Dudley rose to his feet, 'I don't think you need to worry much about Hardin pawing sand. I've a notion recent events have shaken him considerably, and that he's getting a glimmer of light on what his animosity toward the cattlemen is to a certain extent responsible for. It isn't pleasant for an honest man to realize that he may have, if even indirectly, caused the death of other honest men. He may squawk a bit, but I feel safe in saying he'll soon cool down.'

*   *   *

The following day, Tom Dudley was conspicuous by his absence.

176

'I don't know where in blazes he went,' Walt Vibart told Hatfield. 'He rode off early this morning and didn't say where he was going. Hope he isn't getting himself into trouble somehow.'

'I expect he is, but he'll live through it, as lots of other folks have,' Hatfield predicted. He sauntered out, leaving Vibart scratching his head.

A little after noon Hatfield saddled up and rode north. He did not follow the trail but jumped Hardin's wire and took the shorter route to the big farmhouse.

A number of Hardin's *vaqueros* were standing about the yard in groups conversing together in low tones when Hatfield rode up. They nodded cordially but did not otherwise address him. Pedro, the old foreman and major-domo, met him on the veranda as he mounted the steps.

'Buenos dias, Capitan,' Pedro greeted gravely. *'El patron* is in the temper most evil.'

'Wouldn't be surprised if he is,' Hatfield chuckled and passed through the door.

In the big living room, old John was pacing back and forth like a caged lion, snorting and fuming. Pedro had not exaggerated; Hardin was indeed in a temper most evil. He glared at Hatfield.

'Something wrong, sir?' the Lone Wolf asked innocently.

'Something wrong? I'll say there's

something wrong!' bellowed Hardin. 'Here I decided the danged cattlemen didn't steal my cows and am all ready to forgive 'em their natural cussedness, and what happens? One of the dad blamed horned toads goes and steals my daughter! Read this, will you?'

He snatched a creased sheet of paper from the table and thrust it under Hatfield's nose. The Ranger managed to keep his face straight but couldn't keep the grin out of his eyes as he read.

Dear Dad: Tom Dudley and I are going to get married this morning. Won't you wish us happiness? We'll be back later, to be forgiven.

Love,
Verna

'Well,' smiled Hatfield, 'all set to forgive them?'

'Forgive 'em!' howled Hardin. 'I'll shoot him and disown her!'

'She'd make a pretty widow all right,' Hatfield conceded gravely, 'but it wouldn't be a nice thing to do.'

Old John began to sputter and swear, but Hatfield interrupted him with a change of subject that commanded his attention.

'Didn't you tell me once, sir, that the girl you once figured to marry and didn't, Eve Gregory, had red hair?'

'Why—why, yes,' Hardin replied in astonishment. 'Red as a sunset. What the devil of it?'

'And,' pursued Hatfield, 'I believe you mentioned once that Tom Dudley reminded you a lot of somebody you'd once known, so much so that at first you thought you actually knew him?'

'That's right,' Hardin admitted. 'Every time I see the young hellion I get a feeling I ought to know him. What the devil you getting at, anyhow?'

'And,' concluded Hatfield, 'the man Eve Gregory ran off with was called Judd, I believe you said, the only name you knew him by. Well, the boys down to the Lazy D and the Lucky Seven call Tom Dudley 'Judd,' a common nickname for Dudley.'

Old John's knees seemed to give way under him and he slumped into a chair.

'Judd—Eve Gregory—red hair!' he mumbled. 'By gosh, that is who the danged young whippersnapper reminds me of. Eve Gregory's son, sure as blazes!

'But that makes it all the worse!' he stormed.

Hatfield smiled down at the angry old man.

'John,' he said, 'come to think of it, don't you figure you owe Eve Gregory a whopping debt of gratitude?'

'Debt of gratitude!' repeated Hardin in scandalized tones. 'Debt of gratitude! Why

179

that blasted hussy . . .'

'Hold it,' Hatfield interrupted. 'I think you do. Because Eve Gregory turned you down, you met and married your Mary, with whom you lived mighty happily, I seem to remember you saying.'

A change came over Hardin's angry face. His snapping eyes turned a trifle misty, and his stern old mouth became wonderfully sweet and tender.

'We were mighty happy together,' he said, his gaze fixed on the mantlepiece across the room.

'And,' Hatfield said softly, his deep voice all music, 'don't you think Mary's daughter has a right to be happy, too?

'Also,' he added with a chuckle, 'think what a fine revenge you'll be getting on Eve. Now Verna will lead Tom Dudley around by the nose for the next forty years, just as she's been leading you for the last twenty.'

Hardin's head jerked up; he stared at the tall Ranger whose steady eyes were now all kindness.

'Hatfield,' he complained querulously, ' you have the dangdest way of putting things, but somehow they always seem to make sense!' He chuckled creakily.

'That's right,' he added. 'Let him put up with her dratted temper for a while and see how he likes it!'

'But why did it have to be a blasted

cattleman!' he grumbled, peevishly.

Jim Hatfield's sternly handsome face underwent a sudden change. It turned bleak as chiselled granite. The sunny green left his long eyes and they became icy gray. His voice, all the music gone from it, shot brittle, evenly spaced words at the farmer.

'Listen, Hardin,' he said, 'because of your insane and utterly unreasonable hatred of cattlemen and your stubborn mulishness, you very nearly precipitated a bloody range war in which, good men would have died for no good reason. Because of your attitude and the similar attitude of the equally foolish ranchers to the south, men have died. Your snarling and snapping at each other and blaming one another for everything that went wrong in the section enabled a smart, salty and utterly ruthless outlaw to slide in and take over. We've had about enough of that kind of foolishness.'

He was fumbling with a cunningly concealed secret pocket in his broad leather belt as he spoke. He laid something on the table in front of Hardin.

Old John stared unbelievingly at the object, a gleaming silver star set on a silver circle, the feared and honored badge of the Texas Rangers. He raised his eyes to Hatfield's face.

'A—a Ranger!' he gulped. 'You're a Texas Ranger!'

His eyes suddenly blazed with excitement and he leaped to his feet. 'And I got you placed

181

at last, too!' he exclaimed. I knew you always reminded me of somebody I'd heard a lot of things about. You're the Lone Wolf!'

'I've been called that,' Hatfield admitted quietly.

'The Lone Wolf!' Hardin repeated dazedly. 'The top Ranger of them all! Well, I'll be darned.' He stared at Hatfield, almost in awe.

'Captain McDowell sent me over here to straighten out this mess, and I aim to do it,' Hatfield resumed. 'Yes, you stirred up a fine kettle of brimstone and fire. And if you and the cattlemen hadn't been so busy glaring at each other across your infernal wire, Ellis Gault wouldn't have been able to move in and feather his nest like he's been doing for the past six months.'

'Ellis Gault!' Hardin gasped. 'Why—why I never knew a nicer feller.'

'Yes, Ellis Gault,' Hatfield repeated. 'Everybody's friend. Chock full of charm and personality, and he played them to the hilt. Characteristics not uncommon to certain of his kind. Plenty of honest folks were ready to swear by Sam Bass. Ben Thompson had many friends among people who should have known better. And there were those who maintained that Billy the Kid was just a poor, misunderstood boy, instead of recognizing him for the cold-blooded killer and thief he was.

'And Gault isn't satisfied with the rich pickings he's been having as cow thief and stage robber. He wants Escondida Valley. He planned a range war, and had it not been for a fortunate series of events, he would have gotten one. A war that would have desolated the valley. Remember the Lincoln county war over in New Mexico? To the last man they fought it out! That is very likely what would have happened in Escondida Valley if Gault had gotten away with it. And he would have gotten away with it had he not made a few of the little slips the owlhoot brand always makes sooner or later. I'm not certain, of course, but I've a notion that either he or his sidekick Preston recognized me for a Ranger. I have a vague feeling that I've seen Preston somewhere before which doubtless would mean that he saw me. Anyhow, Gault seemed to sort of go off half-cocked and did some foolish things. Which eventually started me to thinking seriously about him. Now I've got the lowdown on him that convinces me he's the man I'm after.'

'Going to arrest him?' Hardin asked.

Hatfield smiled a little ruefully. 'Wish I could, but I can't,' he replied. 'Not yet. I haven't anything on him that would stand up in court. A smart lawyer would get him off in no time. But I believe I can lay a trap he'll walk into, with your help.'

'You'll get it,' Hardin instantly promised. I don't know what you've got on Gault, but your word is good enough for me. I'm with you till

183

the last brand is run.'

'I'll tell you what I know and you can judge for yourself,' Hatfield said.

At that moment a clatter of hoofs sounded outside, followed by a storm of startled exclamations from the *vaqueros*. Steps mounted the veranda. Verna appeared in the doorway, her pretty face a trifle apprehensive, but with her round little white chin firmly set. Behind her loomed Tom Dudley, looking more than a trifle apprehensive.

'Hello, Dad,' Verna greeted her father. 'You know my husband, don't you?'

Old John did not turn a hair. 'Sure I know him,' he rumbled. 'Come in, Dudley, and take a load off your feet. And you run along upstairs for a while, chick, us men have got business matters to talk over.'

CHAPTER EIGHTEEN

After a thoroughly dazed Verna had departed, and an equally dazed Dudley had sunk into a chair, Hatfield briefly outlined what he had discovered on the cliff top, with a brief summary of what he had already told Hardin, to prepare Dudley for what was coming.

'Smart,' rumbled old John, 'darn smart. That hellion has plenty of wrinkles on his horns.'

'Yes, he's not short on savvy,' Hatfield agreed. 'I've a notion maybe he got the idea from watching stock ships load horses and cattle at Brownsville and Port Isabel, down at the mouth of the Rio Grande. They employ a similar shears and windlass method. A procedure made to order for him, for it's doubtful if any rancher or cowhand in the valley ever saw a stock ship loaded and such a method of getting the cows out of the valley would never have occurred to them.

'You're right there,' agreed Hardin. 'I know I never saw it done.'

'Me, neither,' said Dudley. 'I always thought they just walked 'em up a plank.'

'But Gault, of course, is thoroughly familiar with the method,' Hatfield added. 'I understand he originally hailed from the lower Rio Grande country.'

'That's right, Willacy county, I've heard him speak of folks I know down there,' said Hardin. 'He said he owned a little spread there. Maybe he did. How do you figure to trap the sidewinder, Hatfield?'

'I'll tell you my plan,' Hatfield replied. 'First, everything must be kept a dead secret. As I told you, John, I've a notion Gault and his bunch are getting jittery. Let them get an inkling of what's in the cards and they'll slide out of the section pronto, or cover up so effectively it will be impossible to pin anything on them. We've got to move quietly and not let any more people in on the secret than absolutely necessary. Tom, I'll deputize your hands and some of John's *vaqueros* to form a posse. About a dozen good men should be enough. I don't think there's more than a dozen or so in Gault's outfit, at the outside. But I want to warn everybody right now, I don't think they'll give up without a fight, even though we get the jump on them, as I expect to. Take that into consideration when you pick your men.'

'You can count on my boys, as many as you want,' growled Hardin.

'And that goes for the Lazy D hands,' added Dudley.

'Okay, so that angle's taken care of,' Hatfield said. 'Now, Tom, here's your chore: Of course, everybody knows that Hardin and the cattlemen have signed a truce, as it were. It's pretty well agreed that the stolen cows don't go over Hardin's land, so they must go through the wide south mouth of the valley. Hammer that point home. Don't tell folks any more than you have to, but talk them into putting every available hand to patrolling the south end of the valley, and see that the word gets around so that it's common knowledge. That should give Gault and his bunch a false feeling of security. And I think you'd better let Sam Lawson in on what's up. He lost three men the other night and is itching to even the score, and he's got it coming to him. Besides he's part owner of the Lucky Seven and has all the say as to what is done there. I'll need him to help with another angle. We'll take up the other details after I've done a little scouting around the trail and the cliffs. Okay, got your powders?'

Hardin and Dudley moved with speed to put Hatfield's plan in operation. Dudley rode down the valley and talked convincingly to the various spread owners. As a result, the south end of the valley swarmed with punchers patrolling the wide mouth with ready rifle and sixgun. Meanwhile the Lazy D and the Lucky Seven, working together, were rounding up a shipping herd, working slowly and selecting only the very best stock. The collected cows were enclosed in a temporary corral on an outlying pasture and were not guarded at night, every available man being openly assigned to patrol duty.

Jim Hatfield scouted the section about the cliff where the hoisting apparatus was hidden. A few hundred yards to the north, where the trail curved sharply around a bulge and was hidden from view by a belt of thicket on the east, he located a point where the cliff was comparatively low, not more than twenty feet. Strong wooden ladders were constructed, slipped down from Hardin's place under cover of darkness and concealed in the thicket.

Four of Hardin's *vaqueros*, men of proven courage and excellent shots, with Hardin himself, Hatfield, Dudley, Sam Lawson and four Lazy D cowboys, including Walt Vibart, made up the posse. After the herd in the corral had gained sizeable proportions, the posse, well after dark, rode to the cliffs, concealed their horses in the thicket and swarmed up the ladders. All night they lay hidden in the growth, to descend and return to the ranchhouse the following morning before it was light.

Day after day the shipping herd in the corral grew, and night after night nothing happened.

Tom Dudley grew pessimistic. 'Do you really think they'll fall for it, Jim?' he asked Hatfield. It looks to me like they've gotten suspicious or something.'

'Don't see any reason why they would have, and I still believe they will fall for it,' Hatfield insisted. 'that herd is growing more valuable all the time. And from Gault's way of looking at things, the set-up is perfect. The cows unguarded, everybody riding the south end of the valley and concentrating on the rougher east half. I'd say they're just waiting until they figure there are all the cows in that corral they can possibly handle. They'll think with everything arranged so nicely for them that they can risk more than the usual number. Just take it easy and wait.'

'I hope there won't be much more waiting,' grumbled Hardin. 'This camping out every night is hard on old bones.'

The following night the sky was somewhat overcast, and although there was a moon, it cast but a dim and illusive light.

'Perfect for the sidewinders,' Hatfield said as they holed up on the cliff top. 'I've a hunch this is it. Be sure your guns are in working order. I'm willing to bet you'll need them before the night is over. And cover that bundle of oil-soaked brush with the tarpaulin we brought along, don't want it to get wet. We'll need all the shooting light we can get when the shindig starts.'

Hatfield's confidence was infectious. The posse became tense and watchful, while the darkness deepened, with a continual threat of rain.

But as a couple of hours dragged tediously by and it was past ten o'clock, and the long slope remained devoid of sound or motion, the enthusiasm waned.

'Just another lost night's sleep,' Hardin grumbled. 'I got a crick in my back and a sciatica pain in my left leg. I'll end up bed-ridden for a month.'

And then a faint sound drifted to the weary watchers. A rhythmic clicking that steadily loudened.

'Horses!' Hatfield breathed 'Coming down the slope. Get set, everybody, but hold your fire till I give the word. We're peace officers and must announce ourselves.'

'The hellions get all the breaks,' fumed Sam

Lawson. 'We'd just ought to mow 'em down from cover as soon they show.'

'Isn't the way of law and order,' Hatfield whispered back. 'Don't forget, when you do that there's always a possibility of making a mistake you'll regret all your life. Shut up, now, they're getting close.'

He stood up, facing where the trail ended at the cliff edge. His face was set in hard lines, his eyes coldly gray. On his broad breast gleamed the star of the Rangers.

Louder and louder grew the sound of approaching horses, their irons scraping and clanking on the stones.

'A dozen, maybe more,' Hatfield muttered. 'We haven't got a man to spare.'

He moved closer to where Tom Dudley crouched beside the heap of oiled brush, a match ready in his hand.

The clatter of approaching hoofs was almost upon them now. Abruptly the horses scraped to a halt. There was a sound of voices speaking in low tones. A light flashed up as a lantern was lighted, and another. By the glow they could see shadowy forms moving about near the edge of the cliff.

Tensely, Hatfield waited. It was necessary that the outlaws get their hoisting apparatus in place, supplying the indubitable evidence he needed for an open-and-shut case. He sensed the posse chafing with impatience behind him, but he had briefed them well on what they were to do and had little fear of an impulsive premature move.

He watched the shears lifted and lashed into place against the notched tree trunks. The windlass was hauled into position, the cable reeved over the pulley and dangled down tile face of the cliff. He reached over and touched Dudley on the shoulder.

The carefully shielded match scratched. There was an instant of tingling suspense. Then with a roar the oil reeking brush caught fire and a sheet of flame soared into the air, making the scene as bright as day.

For a moment the outlaws grouped around the hoisting contrivance stood as if paralyzed. Jim Hatfield's voice rang out above the clatter of startled exclamations, 'In the name of the state of Texas! Gault, Preston, you are under arrest. Anything you say . . .'

Tate Preston screamed with fear and fury. 'I told you he was a goddam Ranger!' he howled. 'Shoot him! Shoot him!'

Preston's maniacal screech shattered the stupor that gripped the outlaws. Shouting and cursing, they went for their guns.

Instantly the posse opened fire, the reports blending in a veritable drumroll of sound.

Four of the rustlers went down under that first blazing volley, but the others fought back with the ferocity of despair. A *vaquero* pitched sideways to lie moaning and gasping. Another fell writhing into the brush, gripping his bullet torn leg. Walt Vibart reeled back, his face visored with scarlet.

Shooting with both hands, Hatfield leaped forward. A fifth outlaw went down under his guns. An answering shot ripped through his sleeve, another burned a red streak along his neck. He fired again and still another rustler pitched forward on his face.

From the cursing, yelling, shooting tangle burst a great blue horse. Straight for the cliff edge he charged and soared over the ragged lip.

'It's Gault' roared Hardin. 'He'll break his neck!'

He didn't. The big moros hit the trail with a crash of hoofs, caught his footing and sped south at a dead run, his rider bending low as lead whistled all about him.

'The hellion's getting away!' bellowed Sam Lawson, pulling trigger as fast as he could.

Jim Hatfield bounded to the cliff edge, shoving his guns into their holsters. One stayed in place, but the other slipped from his hand and fell to the ground. Without waiting to retrieve it, he gripped the dangling rope and slid down so fast his hands were scorched and blistered when he hit the ground. He raced to where he had left Goldy and swung into the saddle.

'Now it's up to you, feller,' he told the sorrel. 'Trail!'

Goldy instantly responded, his irons

drumming the surface of the trail.

'Easy!' Hatfield cautioned. 'Don't run yourself out. It's going to be a long chase, but we'll get the sidewinder, feller, we'll get him!'

Goldy leveled off in a steady gallop. His nostrils whistled as the breath exhaled from his great lungs. He snorted, slugged his head above the bit and stretched his long legs.

Hatfield felt sure that Gault, confident in the speed and endurance of his splendid mount, would stick to the trail, heading straight for the valley mouth, beyond which lay the rugged hill country, the Rio Grande and safety. In fact, it was doubtful if at the moment he feared any serious pursuit. He would reason that the posse, their hands full with the fight on the cliff top, would be slow getting under way. He had a nice head start, and everything was in his favor.

'But he didn't figure on you, feller,' Hatfield told Goldy. 'Sift sand, jughead, we'll sight him any time now.'

They did, a half hour later, topping the crest of a rise more than a half mile distant and travelling fast. Hatfield settled himself for a gruelling chase.

But when he again caught sight of the fugitive just going over the crest of a second rise, Goldy had cut the half mile to a little more than a quarter. He encouraged the great sorrel with voice and hand.

'We're doing it, feller! We're doing it!'

For a third time he caught sight of the fleeing outlaw, but now Gault was glancing over his shoulder. He realized he was being pursued and was urging the moros to give everything he had. Hatfield could see the flash of his quirt as he lashed the blue horse unmercifully.

The moros was giving his best, but it wasn't enough. Slowly but surely Goldy closed the distance. The quarter-mile dwindled to four hundred yards, shrank to three. Hatfield could see the white blur of Gault's face outlined in the wan light as he repeatedly glanced over his shoulder. A little more and he would be within shooting range, and overhead the sky was clearing.

The trail ran under an overhang of the cliff and was shadowy. Hatfield lost sight of his quarry. Leaning forward in the saddle he strove to pierce the gloom ahead. He flashed around a bulge of cliff, and there was Gault sitting his sobbing, utterly winded horse and waiting for him. He jerked Goldy to a sliding halt as the outlaw opened fire.

It was almost blind shooting in the vague uncertain light. Hatfield heard the whistle of lead zipping past his face, felt its hot burn along his ribs. He answered the outlaw, shot for shot, paused to take deliberate aim, and heard the hammer of his gun click on an empty shell. Instantly he hurled himself sideways from the saddle, gripping the stock of his

194

Winchester as he went down. His life depended on the rifle coming smoothly out of the boot. If it stuck he would be dead in three seconds.

The long gun caught, resisted, tore free. Prone on the ground, Hatfield flung it forward underhand and pulled the trigger.

Gault reeled as the heavy bullet caught him squarely in the middle. Hatfield fired again and the second slug crossed the first in Gault's body. He slumped forward and slid slowly to the ground, to lie writhing and twitching.

Hatfield got to his feet and walked forward, cocked rifle at the ready, but when he reached Gault, the outlaw chief was dead. For a moment he stood gazing down at him.

Why, he wondered, did a man given all the qualities necessary to make an outstanding success of life have to throw it away riding a crooked trail? With a shake of his head he turned and walked stiffly to his horse. Mounting, he turned the sorrel and rode slowly back up the trail.

The posse had descended from the cliff top and were waiting at its base when Hatfield rode into view. They raised a shout of welcome and John Hardin came hurrying forward.

'Get him?' he asked eagerly. 'Good! Preston's dead, too, and so are half a dozen others. We got four prisoners. No, none of our boys were killed. Lopez has a hole through his shoulder and Estaban one through his leg. I patched 'em up and they can ride. Vibart got a chunk of meat knocked off the side of his head but he can still cuss. Sam Lawson got drilled through the arm and is cussing better than ever. Here's your hogleg you dropped up top the cliff. What'll we do with the prisoners?'

'We'll take them to the Lazy D bunkhouse and put a guard over them till morning,' Hatfield replied. 'Tomorrow we'll run them up to Marton and turn them over to the sheriff. Did they have anything to say?'

'Yes, they talked, after somebody suggested it would be a notion to put that rope hanging down the cliff to good use,' Hardin answered grimly. 'You were right about everything, son. Gault did get the idea of lifting the cows out of the valley from watching cattle ships load over at Port Isabel, years ago. He owned a little spread there. Sold out and went to Arizona where he tied up with Preston. He had a record that beat all, I gather. Arizona got a bit hot for them and they came over here. Gault decided this would be a good section to squat in, so he got title to some land and set up as an honest rancher. Maybe he figured to go straight, in the beginning, but I guess he couldn't resist the good pickings to be had hereabouts, or maybe his bunch of hellions prodded him into it. Then he got ambitious as the devil and figured, just as you said, to take over the whole valley and be the biggest cattleman in this end of the state. And if it hadn't been for you, son, I've a notion he would have done it.'

'Maybe,' Hatfield conceded. 'Never can tell how things might work out. Well, suppose we get going. I could use something to eat and a little sleep. Then I've got to be riding. Captain Bill will have another chore lined up for me, the chances are, by the time I get back to the post.'

Jim Hatfield was in a very contented frame of mind as he rode north two days later. In beautiful Escondida Valley he was leaving sunshine and peace. He paused at the big white farmhouse, where Verna and Tom Dudley were spending a few days, to say goodbye to old John. Then he rode on, tall and graceful atop his great golden horse, to where duty called and new adventure waited.

Verna's blue eyes were dreamy as she gazed after his departing form.

'Something to remember,' she murmured softly.

'You're darn right,' agreed Dudley. 'Nobody will ever forget him!

We hope you have enjoyed this Large Print book. Other Chivers Press or G.K. Hall & Co. Large Print books are available at your library or directly from the publishers.

For more information about current and forthcoming titles, please call or write, without obligation, to:

Chivers Press Limited
Windsor Bridge Road
Bath BA2 3AX
England
Tel. (01225) 335336

OR

G.K. Hall & Co.
P.O. Box 159
Thorndike, Maine 04986
USA
Tel. (800) 223-2336

All our Large Print titles are designed for easy reading, and all our books are made to last.